The ESL Reader's Companion to

The House on Mango Street

Linda Butler

The McGraw-Hill Companies, Inc.

New York St. Louis San Francisco Auckland Bogotá
Caracas Lisbon London Madrid Mexico Milan Montreal
New Delhi San Juan Singapore Sydney Tokyo Toronto

This book is dedicated with love to my parents, Jane and Paul Butler.

McGraw-Hill
A Division of The **McGraw·Hill** Companies

The ESL Reader's Companion to *The House on Mango Street*

Copyright © 1996 by The McGraw-Hill Companies, Inc. All rights reserved. Printed in the United States of America. Except as permitted under the United States Copyright Act of 1976, no part of this publication may be reproduced or distributed in any form or by any means, or stored in a database or retrieval system, without the prior written permission of the publisher.

4 5 6 7 8 9   QWF QWF   0 5 4 3

ISBN 0-07-009429-2

Sponsoring editor: Tim Stookesberry
Production supervisor: Natalie Durbin
Project management: Fritz/Brett Associates
Copy editor: Susan Defosset
Cover design: Elizabeth Williamson
Interior design: Rogondino & Associates
Compositor: Pat Rogondino
Illustrator: Katherine Tillotson
Printer and binder: Quebecor Printing Fairfield, Inc.

Library of Congress Catalog Card Number 99-75133

Information has been obtained by The McGraw-Hill Companies, Inc. from sources believed to be reliable. However, because of the possibility of human or mechanical error by our sources, The McGraw-Hill Companies, Inc., or others, The McGraw-Hill Companies, Inc. does not guarantee the accuracy, adequacy, or completeness of any information and is not responsible for any errors or omissions or the results obtained from use of such information.

From THE HOUSE ON MANGO STREET by Sandra Cisneros. Copyright © 1984 by Sandra Cisneros. Published by Vintage Books, a division of Random House, Inc., New York and in hardcover by Alfred A. Knopf, Inc. in 1994. Reprinted by permission of Susan Bergholz Literary Services, New York. All Rights Reserved.

The interview with Sandra Cisneros is from INTERVIEWS WITH WRITERS OF THE POST-COLONIAL WORLD conducted and edited by Feroza Jussawalla and Reed Way Dasenbrock. Reprinted by permission of University Press of Mississippi.

All dictionary entries from THE NEWBURY HOUSE DICTIONARY OF AMERICAN ENGLISH that appear in this book are reprinted by permission. Copyright © 1996 by Heinle & Heinle Publishers, an International Thomson Publishing Company.

CONTENTS

Preface v
To the Student viii

Starting Out 1
PART ONE: The House on Mango Street; Hairs;
    Boys & Girls; My Name 3
About Quoting 21
PART TWO: Cathy Queen of Cats; Our Good Day; Laughter;
    Gil's Furniture Bought & Sold; Meme Ortiz 23
PART THREE: Louie, His Cousin & His Other Cousin; Marin;
    Those Who Don't; There Was an Old Woman She Had So
    Many Children She Didn't Know What to Do; Alicia Who
    Sees Mice; Darius & the Clouds 39
TEST YOURSELF - Vocabulary Review for Parts 1 and 2 55
PART FOUR: And Some More; The Family of Little Feet;
    A Rice Sandwich; Chanclas 59
PART FIVE: Hips; The First Job; Papa Who Wakes Up Tired in
    the Dark; Born Bad; Elenita, Cards, Palm, Water 75
TEST YOURSELF - Vocabulary Review for Parts 3 and 4 89
PART SIX: Geraldo No Last Name; Edna's Ruthie; The Earl
    of Tennessee; Sire; Four Skinny Trees 93
PART SEVEN: No Speak English; Rafaela Who Drinks
    Coconut & Papaya Juice on Tuesdays; Sally; Minerva
    Writes Poems; Bums in the Attic 105
TEST YOURSELF - Vocabulary Review for Parts 5 and 6 117
PART EIGHT: Beautiful & Cruel; A Smart Cookie; What
    Sally Said; The Monkey Garden; Red Clowns 119
PART NINE: Linoleum Roses; The Three Sisters; Alicia & I
    Talking on Edna's Steps; A House of My Own;
    Mango Says Goodbye Sometimes; About the Author 135
TEST YOURSELF - Vocabulary Review for Parts 7, 8, and 9 146
Afterword 149
Answer Key 152
Teaching Suggestions 157
Words to Know 163

PREFACE

The ESL Reader's Companion to The House on Mango Street is a workbook and guide that will help ESL/EFL students to understand and enjoy the novel, and will enhance their language learning as they do so.

The *Companion* is appropriate for students in university, secondary school, or adult ESL programs. It offers the support needed especially by students who:

- Have not yet read extensively in English, or
- Do not usually read for pleasure in their first language, or
- Are making the transition from materials written expressly for learners of English.

Full-length novels present an excellent resource for learners of English. Novels expose students to a great quantity of authentic written English where the language is true to a particular setting and particular relationships. Literature can provide the basis for lively discussion, thoughtful writing, vocabulary building, and cultural understanding— along with all the pleasures of a good story!

The House on Mango Street, by award-winning author Sandra Cisneros, is a novel written as a series of vignettes through which we come to know the world of Esperanza Cordero, a young Mexican-American girl growing up in a poor Chicago neighborhood. Esperanza speaks to us in language that is simple, and therefore accessible to learners of English, yet it is a deceptive simplicity, for so much bubbles beneath the surface of her words. Cisneros said of this book,

> I wanted to write a series of stories that you could open up at any point. You didn't have to know anything before or after and you would understand each story like a little pearl, or you could look at the whole thing like a necklace. (Feroza Jussawalla and Reed Way Dasenbrock, *Interviews with Writers of the Post Colonial World* [Jackson, MS: University Press of Mississippi, 1992], 305)

The stunning "necklace" she created offers learners of English a wealth of material for reflection, for discussion in class, and for writing of their own.

This *Companion* can be used with any edition of the novel, but the page numbers given in it refer to the Vintage Books edition (ISBN 0-679-73477-5) published by Vintage Books, a division of Random House, Inc., of New York.

ORGANIZATION OF THE *COMPANION*

The *Companion* begins with before-the-novel discussion questions ("Starting Out"). Each of the nine *Companion* chapters that follow contains several sections:

Before You Read

This section contains cultural information, translations of words written in Spanish, and explanations of words or expressions that may be uncommon, so students need not waste time hunting for them in their dictionaries. Like any novel with realistic dialogue, *The House on Mango Street* includes language that is inappropriate for students' own use.

On Your Own

This section contains basic comprehension questions about characters and events as well as questions that ask for readers' personal opinions. It ends with an invitation to students to write any questions they would like to ask the instructor about the novel.

Discussion

This section provides more challenging questions about the novel. Some questions send readers delving into the text to analyze it, to synthesize information, and to find support for their opinions. Other questions address issues raised by the novel and ask readers to share their thoughts.

Scene from the Novel

On pages 65 and 138 you will find instructions for dramatizing conversations in the novel. Students can create scripts to read aloud.

Suggestions for Writing

Each of the three elements in this section will further students' understanding of the reading and help develop their English writing skills.

Personal Response Students can keep a journal in which they comment on whatever they choose about the story.

Summarizing Students can develop their skills at writing summaries through a variety of exercises.

Points of Departure The topics given here are based on themes and events from the novel. Some focus on the novel itself, others on personal experiences.

Words to Know

From each part of the novel, ten to sixteen words or expressions have been chosen that are important for students to know. These words may be:

- Essential to understanding a key element in the novel,
- Familiar to students as having one meaning but used differently in the novel, and/or
- Valuable additions to students' general knowledge of English.

The words are presented in the context of sentences about the story. The exercises provide the repeated exposures to words that help learners understand and remember them, plus a mini-review of the story. Answers appear in the Answer Key on page 152.

The *Companion* also includes the following sections:

About Quoting

The conventions of quoting are introduced, followed by practice exercises based on the novel. The instructions to the student show the Modern Language Association format used in U.S. colleges and universities for papers in English and the humanities.

Test Yourself

Each of these sections provides a review of Words to Know studied earlier in the *Companion*. Answers appear in the Answer Key.

Concluding Sections

The *Companion* concludes with an Answer Key, Teaching Suggestions, and a complete list of the Words to Know.

ACKNOWLEDGMENTS

The author wishes to thank many people who helped in the creation of this *Companion:*

Thank you to the ESL teachers and students in Massachusetts who tested the materials and welcomed me into their classes: Pamela Kennedy, Holyoke Community College; Jane Thiefels, Northern Essex Community College; Nancy Concannon, Brighton High School; and Mary Drucker, Salem State College. The author also thanks Frances P. de Cordova, State Literacy Missions Consultant, BGCO (OK); Kara Garrett, Big Bend Community College (WA); and Margaret W. Puck, Palomar College (CA), for reviewing preliminary versions of these materials.

Thanks also to Beatriz Cardenas for translation assistance; Irene Papoulis and Jean Bernard Johnston for their feedback and support; Jane Sloan, godmother to this *Companion;* Margaret Metz and the entire sales and marketing staff of McGraw-Hill for their promotional efforts; and a special thanks to the McGraw-Hill editorial team of Tim Stookesberry, Gina Martinez, Pam Tiberia, Bill Preston, and Thalia Dorwick for their support and guidance.

Above all, the author wishes to thank Sandra Cisneros for writing her wonderful book.

TO THE STUDENT

First of all, congratulations! You have reached a point in your language learning where you are ready to read a novel written for an English-speaking audience. It is quite an accomplishment to have come so far. Now, to help you further along on your way, here is a "Companion."

The aim of this book is to increase your understanding of *The House on Mango Street* and your pleasure in reading it. In addition, it will help you to expand your vocabulary.

So now, let's begin!

STARTING OUT

1. Describe to a partner the kind of house you would like to own. Write down what you like best about your partner's "dream house." Share what you have talked about with a small group or the class.

2. Read the information about the novel on the front and back covers and "About the Author" on page 111.

    - Ask your instructor to explain anything that is not clear to you. As you read, circle any word, phrase, or sentence that makes an impression on you.

    - With a partner or a small group of classmates, read aloud what you circled and explain your reactions.

3. In this novel, you will see almost no quotation marks (" "). Author Sandra Cisneros has chosen not to use them.
   We usually use quotation marks to enclose the words that someone spoke. For example,

    Mary said, "I'll see you later!"

   In the academic writing that you do, it will be important to use quotation marks in the usual way.

   Where would you put quotation marks in the following excerpt from page 13? (Note: There is more than one way to punctuate the last sentence.)

   ### Cathy Queen of Cats

   You want a friend, she says. Okay, I'll be your friend. But only till next Tuesday. That's when we move away. Got to. Then as if she forgot I just moved in, she says the neighborhood is getting bad.

4. Answer this question in writing:

    How do you feel about reading a novel in English?

    Share what you have written and talk about your feelings with a partner or group of classmates.

✑ Part One ✑

The House on Mango Street
Hairs
Boys & Girls
My Name
(pages 3–11)

"... born like me in the Chinese year of the horse..." (10)

BEFORE YOU READ

Take a look at the following words and expressions. They may be new to you, and they may not be in your dictionary.

You *do not* need to memorize these words and expressions, but you *do* need to understand them in the story.

PAGE

3   **Mango** = a tropical tree and its sweet juicy fruit (Mangos are uncommon in the U.S.)

   we were six = there were six people in my family

4   **the flat** = the apartment

   boarded up = having broken windows covered with wooden boards

5   **made me feel like nothing** = made me feel that I had no value or importance

   for the time being = just for now, temporarily

8   **she comes right after me** = she is the next younger child in my family

10   **the Chinese year of the horse** (According to Chinese tradition, each year in a twelve-year cycle is named after a certain creature: the rabbit, the tiger, the dragon, etc. It is said that this creature influences the character of any person born in that year.)

11   **the story goes** = people say

   if she made the best with what she got = if she accepted her fate and did the best that she could with her life

   they say my name funny = they pronounce my name in a strange way

ON YOUR OWN

Reading

Read pages 3–11 *without stopping*.

Try to get the main idea of what is happening in the story without pausing at new words.

When you finish, take out your dictionary and use it as you reread these pages. At this time, you can also begin writing in a reading journal. (See page 9, Personal Response.)

Marking Your Book

Try rereading with pen or pencil in hand. Then you can mark your book—underline words or sentences, or make notes in the margins.

A Closer Look

Write your answers to the following questions in the spaces provided.

The House on Mango Street (pages 3–5)

1. How is the house on Mango Street different from the places where the family lived before?

2. Is Esperanza happy to be living there? Why or why not?

Hairs (pages 6–7)

3. What do you think are Esperanza's feelings about her mother?

4. Have you ever wished that your hair were different? Why or why not?

Boys & Girls (pages 8–9)

5. Why do you think Esperanza's brothers can't let anyone see them talking to girls?

6. When you were a child, did boys and girls "live in separate worlds"? Explain your answer.

7. How old do you think Esperanza is? Why do you think so?

My Name (pages 10–11)

8. Does your given name or your family name have a meaning? If it does, what does it mean?

9. Have you ever changed your name or thought about changing it? If you have, explain why.

10. How does Esperanza feel about her name?

11. What are Esperanza's feelings about her great-grandmother?

Did anything confuse you? Do you want to know more about something in the story?

Write any question you have about the book so far on a separate piece of paper, and give it to your teacher. Your teacher might answer it or might tell you, "Wait—that's coming in the story." Or maybe the answer to your question is something that you must discover for yourself.

DISCUSSION

Through talking with other readers, your ideas about the novel may change. Sometimes your ideas will become more clear to you when you speak about them. And sometimes a classmate will say the same thing you were thinking and make you feel more sure of your ideas.

But in discussion, you might also hear something that makes you see the novel differently. Then you can reread those pages and rethink your ideas.

In some cases, all readers need to get the same information from the novel. But at other times, there can be more than one good interpretation. Novels are like that: readers come to the story with different life experiences and beliefs, so readers can come away from the story each understanding it in a different way.

Some of the questions in the Discussion section of each chapter have one good answer that your group must discover. Other questions can have more than one good answer.

1. How much do you know about Esperanza's family so far?

2. What else would you like to know about them?

3. Esperanza says about her great-grandmother, "I have inherited her name, but I don't want to inherit her place by the window" (11). What does she mean?

4. Esperanza says that "the Chinese, like the Mexicans, don't like their women strong" (10). In your country, do people like women to be strong? Explain your answer.

5. Esperanza described "the house Papa talked about when he held a lottery ticket" (4). Do you buy lottery tickets? Why or why not?

SUGGESTIONS FOR WRITING

Personal Response

Begin a reading journal for *The House on Mango Street*. Keep one notebook or folder just for this purpose.

You can make an entry in your journal after you finish your non-stop reading, or while you are rereading. You can add to an entry after discussion in class.

To make an entry, draw a line down a page in your notebook. To the left of that line, write down anything from the novel that made an impression on you. You can copy words or whole sentences, or you can use your own words. Write down whatever you noticed that you want to comment on.

To the right of the line, write your reaction to what you wrote on the left. Perhaps it confused you or surprised you; perhaps it made you smile or made you angry. Perhaps it reminded you of something, either from your own life or from something else you had read.

Look on the following page for an example of an entry from a reading journal.

Here is what one student, Sophal Chhoun, wrote as a journal entry for Part 1:

What I Noticed	My Reaction
the house that Esperanza dreamed about (page 4)	Everybody has dreams like this, but in reality, it's not going to happen unless you work for it. I had dreams like this when I lived in the refugee camp in Thailand. A dream like that put me in a different place. It helped me carry on.
"Boys & Girls" (pages 8-9)	In my country, when you get to be a teenager, girls are not supposed to talk to boys because of the rules of the society. It also makes a girl's family value go up if they know she doesn't flirt (talk to boys).
"the Chinese, like the Mexicans, don't like their women strong" (page 10)	I think this means Mexican and Chinese men don't want women to be smarter or wiser than they are. Even now there are some men who still think like that. For example, those men want their wives to be housewives. They don't want their wives to lead the family. They want their wives to be like dolls and listen to them. I think it's sexist!

Summarizing

When you write a summary of a story, you retell the story in fewer words, giving only the main points.

Activity 1 Put the following sentences in order to make a summary of "The House on Mango Street" (pages 3–5). Write them as a paragraph.

But the house on Mango Street is not the house they used to talk about, not the house she dreamed about.

In those days, her parents would always talk about the house they were going to own someday.

Before they moved there, they had lived in a series of poor apartments.

It is small and in bad condition, so she is disappointed in it.

In "The House on Mango Street," the narrator describes moving to Mango Street with her family.

Sometimes we use present tense verbs in writing a summary. With present tense verbs, the summary sounds as if the action is happening now. We can do this because a story happens again every time someone new comes to the novel and reads it.

Activity 2   Write the verbs in this summary in the *present*:

Boys & Girls

Esperanza ___*says*___ that boys and girls "_____ in
          (say)   (live)
separate worlds" (8). For example, her brothers, Carlos and

Kiki, _____ to her and her sister Nenny outside the
      (talk, not)
house. Nenny _____ younger than Esperanza _____, so
              (be)   (be)
Esperanza _____ responsible for her.
               (feel)

Sometimes we use past tense verbs in writing a summary. Then the summary sounds as if the story has already happened.

Activity 3   Write the verbs in this summary in the *past*:

My Name

Esperanza ___*got*___ her name from her great-grandmother,
          (get)
"a wild horse of a woman." She _____ so wild that she
                                  (be)
_____ to get married, but Esperanza's great-grandfather
  (refuse)
_____ her marry him. Esperanza _____ that
  (make)   (say)

she _____ a life like her great-grandmother's, a
         (want, not)
life spent looking sadly out the window, and she _____
                                                                    (wish)
she could change her name.

When *you* write a summary of a story, choose present or past and be consistent. Check your verb tenses when you finish.

Points of Departure

Your teacher may ask you to do a writing assignment from the Points of Departure section in your journal, or as freewriting in class, or in the form of an essay.

1. Esperanza defines a "best friend" as someone she can tell secrets to and someone who will understand her jokes without needing any explanation. How would *you* define "a best friend"? Describe at least three things that you think are important in a close friend. Explain why these things are important to you. You can use examples from your own experience to show what you mean.

2. Write about a place (or the place) where you lived as a child. Where was it? What did it look like? How did you feel about it? What did you like most and least about it? Can you still go to this place? Does it seem different to you now than it did when you were a child?

3. How would you describe Esperanza? From what you have read so far, what can you say about her personality, her hopes, and the things that she values?

WORDS TO KNOW

The part of speech for each word is given after the word. What do these abbreviations stand for?

n. = _____   v. = _____   adj. = _____   adv. = _____

Learning New Words

If a word is new to you,
1. Look at the sentence to see how it is used. You can also look back at its use in the novel.
2. Guess at the meaning.
3. Look it up in your dictionary. Were you right?
4. Take notes about the word.

An asterisk (*) marks irregular verbs.

PAGE

3   **broom** *(n.)* They own this house, so there is no landlord to bang on the ceiling with a **broom** if they are noisy.

your notes here →

     even so *(adv.)* They finally have a house of their own, but **even so**, Esperanza doesn't seem very happy about it.

4   **brick** *(n.),* **crumble** *(v.)* The **bricks** in the walls of the house are old and starting to **crumble**.

     swollen *(adj.)* Water makes wood swell, and the wooden front door is so **swollen** that it is hard to open.

14 The ESL Reader's Companion

ordinary *(adj.)* The stairs are **ordinary**, not special in any way.

5   **rob** *(v.)* Somebody broke in and **robbed** the laundromat downstairs from their apartment on Loomis Street.

peel *(v.)* The building needed a new coat of paint. The old paint was **peeling**.

6   **slippery** *(adj.)* Nenny's hair feels smooth and **slippery**.

8   **plenty** *(n.)* In public, the boys don't speak to their sisters, but at home they have **plenty** to say.

pick *(v.)* Esperanza says we can't **pick** our sisters. We have no choice in the matter.

turn out *(v.)* Esperanza thinks Nenny will **turn out** to be like the Vargas kids if she plays with them.

since *(conjunction)* Esperanza says that Nenny is her responsibility **since** Nenny is younger than she is.

10   **sob** *(v.)* Esperanza's father plays Mexican records with songs that sound sad, "songs like **sobbing**."

The House on Mango Street

11 **forgive** *(v.)** People say that Esperanza's great-grandmother never **forgave** her great-grandfather for carrying her off.

inherit *(v.)* Esperanza **inherited** her name from her great-grandmother.

Exercise 1 Write each word or phrase next to its definition.

    a brick   a broom   even so   plenty

1. _____ a long-handled brush for sweeping the floor clean

2. _____ a hard block of baked clay used in building walls, houses, etc.

3. _____ although that is true, nevertheless

4. _____ more than enough

Exercise 2 Use one of the following words or phrases to complete each sentence about the story. Change word forms if necessary.

    crumble   even so   inherit   pick   sob   turn out

1. There are good things about the house on Mango Street, but _____, it is a disappointment to Esperanza.

2. The house on Mango Street is made of bricks. Some of them are in bad condition, and they are _____.
                                                        (-ing)

3. We can't _____ our sisters, Esperanza tells us; we just have to accept the ones we get.

4. Esperanza doesn't want her sister Nenny to be like the Vargas children, and she is afraid that if Nenny plays with them, she'll _____ to be like them.

5. The Mexican records that Esperanza's father listens to must be very sad. She thinks the singers sound as if they are _____.
(-ing)

6. Esperanza was given her great-grandmother's name, so she says that she _____ her name.
(past)

Exercise 3 Use the same words or phrases to complete the following sentences. These sentences do *not* relate to the story, so you will see the words used in other contexts. Change word forms if necessary.

crumble   even so   inherit   pick   sob   turn out

1. You can't choose your relatives, but you can _____ your friends.

2. When I picked up the cookie, it _____, and little pieces of it fell on the table.
(past)

3. Parents pass on characteristics to their children through their genes. For example, we _____ our eye color from our parents.

4. The child was so unhappy about losing her doll that she cried long and hard. Finally, she _____ herself to sleep.

5. The game didn't _____ the way we hoped: our team lost.

6. My vacation was wonderful, but _____, I was glad to get home again.

Exercise 4 Choose the best adjective to complete each sentence about the story.

        ordinary   swollen   slippery

1. The front door to the house on Mango Street sticks and is hard to push open because it is _____.

2. There is nothing special about the stairs in the house. They are just _____.

3. Nenny's hair "slides out of your hand" because it is so smooth and _____.

Exercise 5 What parts of speech are the boldfaced words in the following sentences?

1. When you stop being angry at a person who hurt you, you **forgive** that person.   *verb*

2. Esperanza thinks that her great-grandmother never **forgave** her husband for making her marry him.   _____

3. I wonder if he asked for her **forgiveness**.   _____

4. Perhaps she did not have a **forgiving** nature.   _____

NOUNS	VERBS	ADJECTIVES	ADVERBS
a robber a robbery	rob		

Exercise 6 Look at the chart above for words related to "rob." Use three different forms of "rob" in the following sentences.

1. There was a _____ at the laundromat on Loomis Street.

2. A _____ broke into the laundromat and stole some money.

3. No one saw when the laundromat was _____.

> The verbs "rob" vs. "steal":
>
> We say someone *robs* a person or a place:
>
> Someone **robbed** the bank on Main Street.
>
> They **robbed** the bank of a lot of money.
>
> The bank was **robbed.**
>
> We say someone *steals* a thing or things (from a person or a place):
>
> They **stole** some money.
>
> They **stole** the money from the bank.
>
> The money was **stolen**.

Exercise 7 Look at the box above. Use the appropriate form of "rob" or "steal" in each sentence.

1. Someone _____ the laundromat.

2. They broke into the laundromat and _____ some money.

3. How much money did they _____?

4. How much money was _____?

5. Nobody knows who _____ the laundromat.

6. Have you ever been _____?

> **peel**
>
> a. *(v.)* to take the skin off a piece of fruit or vegetable
>
> b. *(v.)* to loosen, pull away, or fall from a surface
>
> c. *(n.)* the skin of fruit or vegetable
>
> From *The Newbury House Dictionary of American English*

Exercise 8 Look at the box above. Which meaning does "peel" have in the following sentences? Write the letter of the definition next to each sentence.

_c_ 1. Where should I put this banana **peel**?

____ 2. The children helped **peel** some carrots for supper.

____ 3. The paint is **peeling** on the house on Mango Street.

> **since**
>
> a. *(conjunction)* because
>
> b. *(adv., preposition, conjunction)* between a time in the past and now

Exercise 9 Look at the box above. Which meaning does "since" have in the following sentences? Write the letter of the definition next to each sentence.

____ 1. They have been married **since** 1975.

____ 2. I'm not going to the party **since** I haven't been invited!

____ 3. They had a fight, and they haven't spoken **since**.

____ 4. **Since** the rent is going up, we'll have to move.

____ 5. I didn't want to go out **since** it was raining hard.

____ 6. You have been talking on the phone ever **since** dinner!

ABOUT QUOTING

What Is Quoting?

When you answer questions about the story, sometimes you will want to write your answer by copying directly from the book. For example, here is question 11 from page 7:

What are Esperanza's feelings about her great-grandmother?

You could write:

Esperanza says, "I would've liked to have known her, a wild horse of a woman" (11–12).

This would be a good answer. In this answer, you would be *quoting— copying the author's words*. (The numbers in parentheses are the page numbers where the words appear in the book.)

Or you could write:

Esperanza thinks her great-grandmother was very wild, and she likes this idea. She says that she is sorry that she never knew her great-grandmother.

In this answer, you would be *using your own words*.

When Do We Quote?

We use quotations when using words of our own would create a problem. For example, using our own words might:

- Change the author's meaning, or
- Require writing many more words to say the same thing, or
- Mean losing a special effect or image the author has created.

It's good to write answers using your own words. That gives you valuable practice thinking about the reading and using your writing skills.

Sometimes, however, you will want to quote. For example:

> What do Esperanza's parents tell her about the disappointing house on Mango Street?

The best answer to this question would use their exact words:

> Her father says that this house is only "temporary," and her mother also says, "For the time being" (5).

How Do We Quote?

The following rules for quoting follow the format prescribed by the Modern Language Association (MLA):

1. Copy the author's words carefully.
2. Put quotation marks before the first word you copy and after the last word.
3. After the quotation marks, put the page number with parentheses around it.
4. Put a period after the final parenthesis.

For example:

Esperanza says the house is "not the house we'd thought we'd get" (3).

Exercise 1 Answer this question *with a quotation from the novel*: How does Esperanza describe the house she hoped to have?

Exercise 2 Answer this question *using your own words*: What does the house on Mango Street look like?

Part Two

Cathy Queen of Cats
Our Good Day
Laughter
Gil's Furniture Bought & Sold
Meme Ortiz
(pages 12–22)

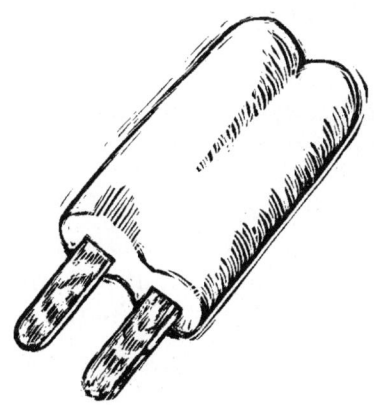

"... Rachel and Lucy who have the same fat popsicle lips..." (17)

BEFORE YOU READ

You *do not* need to memorize these words and expressions, but you *do* need to understand them in the story.

PAGE

12   **She says** (Usually when we write what someone said, we use the *past* tense: "she said." The *present* tense is used (1) in informal spoken and written English, or (2) when someone says something repeatedly, as in: "My mother always says, 'Eat your vegetables.'")

       great great grand cousin = a distant cousin (Cathy has invented this phrase.)

       stuck-up = conceited, with a high opinion of herself

13   **donuts** = doughnuts (small fried cakes in the shape of a circle)

15   **doesn't get it** = doesn't understand it (Lucy doesn't understand that Esperanza is trying to correct Lucy's grammar. Esperanza says, "You mean *she* was born here, not *Her* was born here." But Lucy thinks Esperanza is saying "You mean *she*—not you—is from Texas.")

16   **sassy** = bold, not showing respect

17   **ice cream bells** (In the summer, ice cream trucks travel around city streets to sell ice cream. When they arrive at a park or in a neighborhood, the drivers get people's attention with the sound of small bells.)

19   **a junk store** = a store that sells used things which are usually of little value

20   **marimba** = a musical instrument like a xylophone

       this ain't for sale = this is not for sale (The word "ain't" is non-standard English.)

21   **with the limbs flopping** = with the legs (or arms and legs) moving freely and loosely

22   **lopsided** = with one side lower than the other

A-framed = built in the shape of the letter A

Tarzan = a fictional character, from a novel and movies, who was raised by apes in the African jungles

ON YOUR OWN

Reading

Read pages 12–22 *without stopping.*

Try to get the main idea of the story without pausing when you read new words.

When you finish, take out your dictionary and use it as you reread these pages. At this time, you can make an entry in your reading journal. (See page 30, Personal Response.)

Marking Your Book

You can mark words or sentences by underlining, circling, or highlighting them. But don't write notes between the lines—they can distract your eye when you reread. Instead, make your notes in the margins.

A Closer Look

Cathy Queen of Cats (pages 12–13)

1. What does Cathy talk to Esperanza about?

2. What is your opinion of Cathy?

Our Good Day (pages 14–16)

3. What are two reasons why this is a good day for Esperanza?

4. Read the following excerpt from "Our Good Day." If Esperanza were writing more formally, where would she put in quotation marks? Would she make any other changes?

>   If you give me five dollars I will be your friend forever. That's what the little one tells me.
>   Five dollars is cheap since I don't have any friends except Cathy who is only my friend till Tuesday.
>   Five dollars, five dollars.
>   She is trying to get somebody to chip in so they can buy a bicycle from this kid named Tito. They already have ten dollars and all they need is five more.
>   Only five dollars, she says.
>   Don't talk to them, says Cathy. Can't you see they smell like a broom.
>   But I like them. Their clothes are crooked and old.

Note: There is more than one way to punctuate this excerpt.

5. Imagine that Esperanza is describing this day in an essay for her English class. She wants to use a more formal writing style than she used in "Our Good Day," so she is editing her work:

I ~~don't~~ *didn't* tell them about Nenny just yet. It'~~s~~ *was* too complicated,˄*e*~~E~~specially since Rachel almost put out Lucy's eye about who was going to get to ride it first. But finally we agree˄*d* to ride it together.

Continue changing verbs to the past tense. Also change "you."

Because Lucy has long legs she pedals. I sit on the back seat and Rachel is skinny enough to get up on the handlebars which makes the bike all wobbly as if the wheels are spaghetti, but after a bit you get used to it.

Also change sentence fragments to complete sentences.

We ride fast and faster. Past my house, sad and red and crumbly in places, past Mr. Benny's grocery on the corner, and down the avenue which is dangerous. Laundromat, junk store, drug store, windows and cars and more cars, and around the block back to Mango.

Continue changing verbs to the past and add punctuation.

```
    People on the bus wave. A very fat lady crossing
the street says, You sure got quite a load there.
    Rachel shouts, You got quite a load there too. She
is very sassy.
```

Laughter (pages 17–18)

6. Why did Nenny say, "That's what I was thinking exactly" (18)? Choose the answer below that seems the best, and be ready to explain your choice in class.

____ The house was built in a Mexican style.

____ Esperanza is older, so Nenny agrees with what she says.

____ Nenny wants to defend her sister from Rachel and Lucy's laughter.

____ Nenny doesn't want Rachel and Lucy to know that her sister is crazy.

____ Other:

Gil's Furniture Bought & Sold (pages 19–20)

7. Would you like to go into this store? Why or why not?

8. In this store, what has a powerful effect on Esperanza?

Meme Ortiz (pages 21–22)

9. What is special about the backyard of Meme's house?

Write any questions *you* have about the novel so far. Give them to your teacher.

DISCUSSION

1. Look back at question 4 on page 26. With one or more classmates, compare your changes to the excerpt from "Our Good Day." (Note: There is more than one way to punctuate this excerpt.) Give your reasons for the choices you made.

2. In "Our Good Day," "A very fat lady crossing the street says, You sure got quite a load there" (16). What does she mean?

3. Rachel answers the lady by saying, "You got quite a load there too" (16). What does she mean?

4. Compare your answers to question 6 on page 28. Share your reasons for your answers. Can you agree on the best answer?

5. So far, does Mango Street seem to be a good street to live on? Explain why you think it does or does not.

6. With a partner, choose a phrase, a sentence, or a group of sentences that made an impression on both of you. One of you should read it aloud; then discuss it. In a group, have one partner tell the page number and the place on the page of your selection. That partner then reads it aloud. The other partner explains why the two of you chose it.

SUGGESTIONS FOR WRITING

Personal Response

Make an entry in your reading journal. Here is the entry that one student, Mirka Cuello, made in her journal:

What I Noticed	My Reaction
p. 13 "I'll be your friend But only till next Tuesday. That's when we move away."	This looks funny. Why only until she moves away? I would be her friend forever. In my country I had friends. Then I moved here to Boston, but my friends and I are still friends.
p. 14 "If you give me five dollars I will be your friend forever."	This looks funny too. I would not be somebody's friend only because of five dollars.
p. 14 "Can't you see they smell like a broom."	This sentence is stupid because how can they smell like a broom?
p. 15 Cassandra, Alexis, or Maritza	She wants to change her name. Why? I don't understand.

Summarizing

Write a summary of "Our Good Day." You can begin with this sentence:

Esperanza makes friends with Lucy and Rachel, two sisters who live across the street.

Your summary should include the answers to these questions:

What does Esperanza give them?
What do they do with the money?
What do they do with the bicycle?
How does Esperanza feel?

Points of Departure

1. Write about someone with whom you often played when you were a child. What did you most like to do together? Describe this person, where you played, and the kinds of things you did (or one special favorite activity). How is your relationship with this person now?

2. Meme won the First Annual Tarzan Jumping Contest by jumping from the big tree—and breaking both his arms. Did you ever do anything dangerous when you were young? If so, describe it. Why did you do it? How did you feel afterwards? How do you feel about it now?

3. In what ways does Mango Street seem to be a good place for Esperanza to be living? In what ways does it seem to be a bad place? Use specific details from the book to show what you mean.

   Do you think Esperanza will ever like it there?

WORDS TO KNOW

> **Learning New Words**
> 1. Look at the sentence to see how the word is used.
> 2. Guess at the meaning.
> 3. Look up the word in your dictionary.
> 4. Take notes about the word.

An asterisk (*) marks irregular verbs.

PAGE

12   **grab** *(v.)* Cathy tells Esperanza to keep away from "Joe the baby-**grabber**."

your notes here →

13   **skinny** *(adj.)* Cathy has big cats, small cats, fat cats, and **skinny** cats.

14   **chip in** *(v.)* Rachel asks Esperanza to **chip in** five dollars towards buying a bicycle.

            crooked *(adj.)* Rachel and Lucy aren't dressed neatly; their clothes are on **crooked**.

15   **tug** *(v.)* Cathy **tugs** at Esperanza's arm, trying to pull her away.

            find out *(v.)** Esperanza thinks Nenny will be happy to **find out** that they own a bicycle.

ahead *(adv.)* Rachel is thinking **ahead**, planning how she and the other girls will share the bike.

take turns *(v.)** Instead of **taking turns**, the three girls ride the bicycle together.

16   **load** *(n.)* A fat lady comments to the girls about what a **load** they have on the bike.

17   **right away** *(adv.)* Esperanza says people don't notice **right away** how she and Nenny are alike.

giggle *(n.)* Lucy and Rachel laugh in a shy way. Esperanza compares their **giggle** to the bells of an ice cream truck.

19   **punch** *(v.)* When someone **punches** the couches in Gil's store, dust flies into the air.

aisle *(n.)* There are narrow **aisles** to walk through in the crowded store.

20   **notice** *(v.)* At first, a customer might not **notice** Gil there in the dark.

float *(v.)* Gil's gold-rimmed glasses seem to **float** in the air.

The House on Mango Street

21   **slant** *(v.)* In Meme's house, the floors aren't level. They **slant**.

Exercise 1 Write each word next to its definition.

>   **an aisle   crooked   a load   skinny**

1. _____ twisted or bent, not straight

2. _____ very thin

3. _____ an amount to carry

4. _____ a space for walking, as between seats in a theater or shelves in a store

Exercise 2 Use one of the following words or phrases to complete each sentence about the story. You will need to change the form of one word.

>   **ahead   chip in   find out   grab   right away   take turns**

1. Cathy warns Esperanza to stay away from the man she calls "Joe the baby-_____."

2. Rachel asked Esperanza to _____ five dollars so they would have enough money to buy a bike.

3. When Nenny gets home, she'll _____ that she and Esperanza are part-owners of a bicycle.

4. Rachel is already planning how they are going to share the bicycle in the future. She is thinking _____.

5. Everybody wants to ride the bike, so all three girls get on at the same time. But in the future, they'll _____.

6. When people look at Esperanza and Nenny, it's not immediately clear that they are sisters. People don't see the resemblance between them _____.

Exercise 3 Use the same words and phrases to complete these sentences, which are *not* related to the story. You will need to change the forms of three words.

> **ahead   chip in   find out   grab   right away   take turns**

1. Everybody _____ so that we could buy pizzas for the party.

2. There was one cookie left on the plate, and the two boys both tried to _____ it.

3. I was very happy when the phone call finally came and I _____ that I got the job that I wanted.

4. Some people like fast-food restaurants because they can get their food _____, without waiting.

5. There was only one baseball glove, so the brothers _____ wearing it.

6. Are you an organized person who plans _____, or do you make decisions at the last minute?

Exercise 4 Are the underlined words used as *nouns* or *verbs*?

verb 1. The little girl was too close to the fire so her mother had to grab her.

_____ 2. The thief made a grab for my purse but missed.

_____ 3. The student had a heavy load of books in her bag.

_____ 4. We loaded the shopping cart with enough food for a week.

_____ 5. The little boy wanted his mother's attention, so he gave a tug on her skirt.

_____ 6. Tugboats are small powerful boats that tug big ships into position in a harbor.

_____ 7. Esperanza tells us that Rachel and Lucy giggle.

_____ 8. To Esperanza, their <u>giggle</u> sounds like the bells of an ice cream truck.

Exercise 5 Complete each sentence in the same group with the same word from this list:

        float   **notice**   **slant**   **tug**

1. Balloons _____ in the air.

   Rocks sink in water, but sticks _____.

   Gil's glasses seemed to _____ in the darkness.

2. When a roof _____, rain and snow slide off it.
   (-s)

   Does your handwriting _____ *to the right like this?*

   The floors in Meme's house _____.

3. Nobody _____ when I wore my new glasses.
   (past)

   We gave the landlord a month's _____ that we were moving out.

   In the darkness of Gil's store, people don't _____ the owner right away.

4. I gave the door a _____, but it wouldn't open.

   In the game "_____ of war," two teams hold opposite ends of a rope, and each team tries to pull the other forward.

   Cathy _____ on Esperanza's arm.
   (past)

> **punch**
>
> a. *(v.)* to hit with the fist, strike
>
> b. *(v.)* to make holes
>
> c. *(n.)* a drink made by mixing fruit juices and other ingredients
>
> d. *(n.)* **punch line**: the line that gives the meaning of a joke
>
> From *The Newbury House Dictionary of American English*

Exercise 6 Look at the box above. Which meaning does "punch" have in the following sentences? Write the letter of the definition next to each sentence.

_____ 1. At the party, they served **punch** and cookies.

_____ 2. One man **punched** the other and gave him a bloody nose.

_____ 3. The conductor **punched** my train ticket to show that the ticket had been used.

_____ 4. Why is everybody laughing? Did I miss the **punch** line?

Part Three

Louie, His Cousin & His Other Cousin
Marin
Those Who Don't
There Was an Old Woman She Had So Many
Children She Didn't Know What to Do
Alicia Who Sees Mice
Darius & the Clouds
(pages 23–34)

"... she doesn't want to spend her whole life in a factory or behind a rolling pin" (31–32).

BEFORE YOU READ

PAGE

23   **nylons** = nylon stockings (Nylons were commonly worn by women and teenaged girls in the U.S. from the 1940's until the late 1960's, when pantyhose became more popular.)

        selling Avon = selling cosmetics to friends and neighbors as a representative of the Avon Company

        gotta = (Marin) has got to

24   **pumpkin pah-ay...so am ah-ay** = pumpkin pie...so am I (Marin's pronunciation)

        he honked = he sounded the horn of the car

        flooring that car = pushing the gas pedal to the floor of the car to make it go as fast as possible

        cop = police officer (Use the word "officer," not "cop," in speaking to a police officer.)

26   **P.R.** = Puerto Rico

29   **There Was an Old Woman...** (This is a nursery rhyme:

> There was an old woman who lived in a shoe,
> She had so many children, she didn't know what to do,
> She gave them some broth without any bread,
> She whipped them all soundly, and sent them to bed.)

        Rosa Vargas' kids are...too much = they are outrageous, past the limits of what is acceptable

        how can they help it = how can they avoid being wild and misbehaving

        bologna = an inexpensive processed meat used in sandwiches

        how come = why

30   **playing chicken** = playing a game in which the winner is the one who dares to go the closest to some danger, such as the edge of a roof

        No wonder = It's no surprise that

        his buck tooth = his top front tooth that sticks out over his bottom lip

31   **tortilla** = a thin flat round Mexican bread made from cornmeal or wheat flour

        catch [sight of] the hind legs = get a quick look at the back legs (of a mouse)

ON YOUR OWN

Reading

Read pages 23–34 *without stopping*.

Don't pause at new words—just try to get the main idea of the story.

When you finish, take out your dictionary and use it as you reread these pages. At this time, you can also make an entry in your reading journal.

Marking Your Dictionary

When you look up a word in your dictionary, make a dot with your pen in the margin next to it. Then if you look up a word and find that it already has three dots next to it, memorize it!

The House on Mango Street   **41**

A Closer Look

Louie, His Cousin & His Other Cousin (pages 23–25)

1. What was so exciting about the visit by Louie's other cousin (not Marin)?

2. When everyone asked Louie's cousin where he got the car, he didn't answer. Where do you think he got it?

3. Do you agree or disagree with this statement:

    Esperanza didn't really understand what was happening.

    Explain your answer.

Marin (pages 26–27)

4. What does Marin look like? How does she dress?

5. What does she do every day?

6. What does Marin dream about?

Those Who Don't (page 28)

7. Who is scared to be in Esperanza's neighborhood?

8. Where does Esperanza feel scared?

9. Are there places that you are scared to go to? Describe them and give your reasons for being scared.

10. Do you think there are people who are scared to come into your neighborhood? If so, who?

There Was an Old Woman . . . (pages 29–30)

11. How do you feel about Mrs. Vargas? Check any or all of the following:

    ____ I feel sorry for her.
    ____ I feel upset about her.
    ____ I feel angry at her.
    ____ Other: _____

12. What do you think happened to Angel Vargas?

Alicia Who Sees Mice (pages 31–32)

13. Describe what Alicia does every day.

Darius & the Clouds (pages 33–34)

14. How does Darius surprise Esperanza?

Write any questions *you* have about this part of the book. Give them to your teacher.

DISCUSSION

1. Explain what Esperanza means when she writes, "See. That's what I mean. No wonder everybody gave up" (30).

2. Describe your feelings about Mrs. Vargas and explain why you feel that way.

3. Is Alicia's father supportive of her going to college? Explain your answer.

4. With a partner, imagine a conversation between Alicia and her father. Decide on the place (the kitchen? the room where she studies?) and the time (early morning? late at night?). Take the roles of Alicia and her father and act out the conversation.

5. Do you agree with the following statement?

    Esperanza admires both Marin and Alicia.

    Explain why you do or do not agree.

6. If you are keeping a reading journal, share something you have written. Read aloud what you wrote on the left side of the page under "What I Noticed." Then tell why it made an impression on you and what you thought about it.

SUGGESTIONS FOR WRITING

Personal Response

Sometimes author Sandra Cisneros uses words in surprising combinations. For example, on page 4, she writes about "windows so small you'd think they were holding their breath." Then on page 17, she describes laughter "like a pile of dishes breaking."

Have you noticed any surprising combinations like these? You can record them in your journal entries. Be sure to include your reactions, either in words or in pictures. (Sketches and cartoons make wonderful additions to a reading journal.)

Summarizing

Activity 1 Write a summary of "Louie, His Cousin & His Other Cousin." You can begin this way:

> Louie is a Puerto Rican boy who lives on Mango Street. One day a cousin of his came to visit and brought a lot of excitement.

Your summary should include the answers to the following questions:

Where were Esperanza and some others playing?
What did Louie's cousin drive up in?
What did everyone ask for?
On their seventh trip around the block, what did they hear?
What did Louie's cousin do then?
What happened to the car?
What happened to Louie's cousin?

Activity 2 Read the following summary of "There Was an Old Woman She Had So Many Children She Didn't Know What to Do."

Summary A Rosa Vargas has a lot of wild children. Her husband left, and she can't control the children by herself. They do dangerous things for fun, like playing on the roof. The neighbors on Mango Street warn them not to, but the children have no respect for adults, and they don't listen. So people stop caring about them, even when Angel Vargas tries to fly and has a terrible fall.

Read summaries B and C and think about why they are not as good as summary A.

Summary B There is a poor woman who has a lot of children. I think she has too many. Her children are wild, and they do things that they shouldn't do. They are also disrespectful and rude. In my opinion, this woman really needs help to control them, and I wonder where their father is. Finally, the children end up getting into trouble.

Summary C Mrs. Rosa Vargas is a single mother who is tired all the time. She "cries every day for the man who left" (29). He disappeared without leaving any money for bologna. He didn't leave a note either. The children spit at Mr. Benny when he told them to come down from the roof. One day Angel "dropped from the sky like a sugar donut" (30).

In which summary do you see each of the following problems? Write B or C on the line.

1. ____ The summary is too general; it needs more specific information.

2. ____ The summary has unnecessary details.

3. ____ The writer hasn't explained the main point of the story.

4. ____ The writer has included a personal opinion in the summary.

Points of Departure

1. Read this poem composed by borrowing phrases from the book:

Marin

in the doorway
clicking her fingers
looks at boys and is not afraid

dancing, singing
under the streetlight
waiting for someone to change her life

The phrases in this next poem come from "Hairs":

Mama
My mother's hair,
My mother's hair,
Like little rosettes,
Like little candy circles,
Sweet to put your nose into
When she is holding you,
Holding you and you feel safe.

Create a short poem by borrowing phrases from the book. You can focus on a character, such as Nenny, Alicia, or the Vargas kids, or a place, such as Mango Street or Gil's junk store, or a thing, such as Esperanza's name or the yellow Cadillac. Choose a title for your poem.

2. Esperanza writes about Mango Street, "... we take what we can get and make the best of it" (33). She means that they accept what they cannot change and try to do well with what little they have.

Several proverbs in English advise this approach to life, proverbs such as "Half a loaf is better than none." Think of a proverb from your first language that offers advice about life. Write out the proverb in your first language, translate it, and explain its meaning. Tell whether or not you agree with this proverb and why.

WORDS TO KNOW

An asterisk (*) marks irregular verbs.

PAGE

24   **alley** *(n.)* There was a game of volleyball going on in the **alley** when Louie's cousin drove up.

         automatically *(adv.)* Pressing a button made the car windows roll up **automatically**.

         siren *(n.)* They heard the **sirens** of the police cars.

         take off *(v.)** At the sound of the sirens, Louis' cousin **took off** in the Cadillac.

blur *(n.)* The car moved so fast that it looked like a **blur**.

26   **get to** *(v.)** Marin wants to get a job downtown where she'll **get to** wear nice clothes.

27   **blink** *(v.)* Marin doesn't even **blink** when boys compliment her.

28   **not know (any) better** Some people are scared when they come into Esperanza's neighborhood because they **don't know any better**.

29   **fault** *(n.)* Esperanza feels that it isn't Mrs. Vargas' **fault** that her children are so wild.

dangle *(v.)* The Vargas children like to hang by their knees so they **dangle** upside down.

30   **spit** *(v.)** The Vargas children didn't answer Mr. Benny. They just **spit**.

give up *(v.)** People **gave up** worrying about those children. They stopped trying to keep them safe.

31   **imagine** *(v.)* Alicia's father tells her that she only **imagines** that there are mice.

33   **wise** *(adj.)* Darius, who isn't generally very smart, said a **wise** thing.

   tough *(adj.)* Darius tries to frighten girls. He likes to think he is **tough**.

34   **simple** *(adj.)* Darius made a complex idea sound **simple**.

Exercise 1   Write each word next to its definition.

   an alley   automatic   a blur   a siren   spit

1. _____ able to move or work without a person operating it

2. _____ an image of something that is not seen clearly

3. _____ a narrow street between or behind buildings in a city

4. _____ a device that makes a loud warning sound, such as on a police car or ambulance

5. _____ saliva

Exercise 2   Use one of the following words or phrases to complete each sentence about the story. You will need to change the forms of two words.

   **dangle   get to   give up   not know any better
   simple   take off**

1. Louie's cousin _____ so fast in that Cadillac that the car looked like just a yellow blur.

2. Marin would like a job downtown where she would _____ wear nice clothes to work.

3. Esperanza says that sometimes people drive into her neighborhood by mistake, and they think it's dangerous there because they do _____.

4. The Vargas children like to _____ upside down, hanging by their knees from the branches of trees.

5. Neighbors on Mango Street tried to talk to the Vargas children but they wouldn't listen, so people just _____.

6. Darius pointed up to a fat white cloud and said that was God. Esperanza thought he made something complicated seem _____.

Exercise 3 Use the same words and phrases to complete these sentences, which are *not* related to the story. You will not need to change any word forms.

> dangle   get to   give up   not know any better
> simple   take off

1. My sister likes earrings that _____ from her ears. She likes the way they dance as she moves.

2. Checking the oil in a car isn't difficult; it is really _____.

3. When the little boy spilled his milk, nobody got angry. He's only two years old, so he does _____.

4. Well, it's getting late, so I'd better _____. Bye!

5. Our TV set stopped working last night, so I didn't _____ watch my favorite program.

6. It's very hard for people to _____ smoking when they have been smokers for a long time.

Exercise 4 Use the same word to complete all three sentences in a group.

blink   fault   tough

1. Okay, everybody! Hold still for the camera, smile, and don't _____.

   He ran to the store so fast that he was back in the _____ of an eye.

   Marin is bold enough to look back at boys and not even _____.

2. It was a very _____ exam, but every student passed.

   The steak looked and smelled good, but it was so _____ that he could hardly chew it.

   Darius thinks he is _____, but it doesn't sound as if anyone is afraid of him.

3. Where there is a major _____ in the earth's surface, there are likely to be earthquakes.

   The accident wasn't my _____; the other driver caused it.

   Esperanza says it's not Rosa Vargas' _____ that her children are so wild.

NOUNS	VERBS	ADJECTIVES	ADVERBS
imagination	imagine	imaginary imaginative	imaginatively

> The adjectives "imaginary" vs. "imaginative":
>
> **imaginary** = not real, just imagined:
> As a child, did you worry about **imaginary** monsters under your bed or in your closet?
>
> **imaginative** = having or showing imagination:
> What a great idea! You're so **imaginative**! You always think of **imaginative** solutions.

Exercise 5 Look at the chart above for words related to "imagine," and read the information in the box. Then fill in each blank with the appropriate member of this word family.

1. Alicia's father tells her that she doesn't really see mice. He claims that she only _____ them.

2. According to him, these mice are _____.

3. Does she really see mice, or is it just her _____?

4. Sandra Cisneros is an _____ writer.

The House on Mango Street 53

Exercise 6 Choose the *adjective* or *adverb* form of the word.

automatic   automatically

1. My car has an _____ transmission. This means that I don't have to shift gears because the car does it _____.

imaginative   imaginatively

2. To solve this problem, we need to think _____. We need an _____ solution to the problem.

simple   simply

3. If you _____ follow this recipe, the cookies will turn out to be delicious. I promise you, they are really _____ to make.

wise   wisely

4. His friends consider him a _____ man, so they go to him for advice. But sometimes he _____ refuses to give any!

TEST YOURSELF

VOCABULARY REVIEW FOR PARTS 1 AND 2

1. Choose the phrase from the list below that best completes each statement, and write it in the space provided.

    . ✓. **inherit** her name.

    . . . **pick** their sisters.

    . . . **crumble** in some places.

    . . . **chip in** to buy a bicycle.

    . . . **turn out** like the Vargas children.

    a. Esperanza admires her great-grandmother, but she wasn't happy to *inherit her name.*

    b. The bricks of the house on Mango Street have begun to _____

    c. Esperanza watches out for her sister so that Nenny won't _____

    d. Rachel asks Esperanza to _____

    e. Esperanza writes that people cannot _____

The House on Mango Street 55

2. Find and circle each word in this puzzle. The words are written going from top to bottom, across from left to right, or diagonally from left to right. Write each word you find next to its definition. If you need to, look back at the lists of Words to Know in Parts 1 and 2.

```
M E V T U G S K
X Q L R X R P S
B(S O B)O A P L
R E A B L B R A
O Z D X R Q N N
O P E E L D M T
M F I N D O U T
W N O T I C E M
```

a. <u>S</u> <u>O</u> <u>B</u> = to cry uncontrollably (from Part 1)

b. _ _ _ = to pull hard (from Part 2)

c. _ _ _ = to steal from (2)

d. _ _ _ _ = to take suddenly and roughly (2)

e. _ _ _ _ = a heavy amount of something to carry (2)

f. _ _ _ _ = to come off in small pieces or layers (1)

g. _ _ _ _ _ = a long-handled brush for sweeping floors (1)

h. _ _ _ _ _ = to slope, be at an angle (not level) (2)

i. _ _ _ _ _ _ = to become aware of (2)

j. _ _ _ _ _ _ _ = to learn for the first time, discover (2)

3. Unscramble each of these words. Their definitions follow.

   a. tafol = f l o a t = to stay on top of a liquid or in the air without sinking

   b. slaei = _ _ _ _ _ = a space for walking, as between seats in a theater or shelves in a store

   c. niskyn = _ _ _ _ _ _ = very thin

   d. docokre = _ _ _ _ _ _ _ = not straight

   e. lewslon = _ _ _ _ _ _ _ = grown bigger because of pressure from within

   f. gerfiov = _ _ _ _ _ _ _ = to pardon, no longer be angry with

   g. arrinody = _ _ _ _ _ _ _ _ = common, everyday, not special

4. Answer these questions about the novel:

   a. What is made of brick? _____

   b. Whose hair is slippery? _____

   c. What will the girls take turns doing? _____

   d. Who giggles like the bells of an ice cream truck? _____
   _____

   e. Where did Esperanza punch couches and watch the dust fly?
   _____

The House on Mango Street 57

❧ Part Four ❧

And Some More
The Family of Little Feet
A Rice Sandwich
Chanclas
(pages 35–48)

". . . a powerful bushel basket . . ." (42)

BEFORE YOU READ

PAGE

35   **the Eskimos** = native people of Alaska and northern Canada

36   **cumulus** =

otherwise known as = also called

There's that wide puffy cloud that looks like your face when you wake up (The words "you" and "your" can be used in two ways: (1) specifically, meaning the person(s) spoken to, or (2) impersonally, meaning any person, as in: That cloud "... looks like your [somebody's] face when you [they] wake up ..." This impersonal "you" is informal and conversational.)

37   **yous** = (plural, nonstandard English) you

Cream of Wheat cereal = thick hot breakfast food

frijoles = (Spanish) beans

39   **tamales** = (Spanish) ground meat rolled in steamed cornmeal dough

40   **hopscotch squares** =

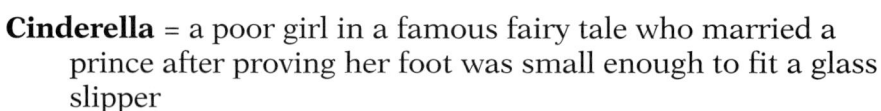

Cinderella = a poor girl in a famous fairy tale who married a prince after proving her foot was small enough to fit a glass slipper

tee-tottering = walking unsteadily

41   **tavern** = a place that serves alcohol, a bar

a bum man = a homeless man with no job

43 **the ones who wear keys around their necks** = children who go home to empty houses after school while their parents are at work (also called "latchkey children")

44 **Spartan** = someone who takes pride in building strength through hard training and in tolerating pain without complaint

anemic = weak and pale

knows. . .by heart = has memorized

Sister Superior = the nun in charge, the school principal

get hollered at = be scolded

45 **three-flats** = three-story apartment buildings

46 **Chanclas** = (Spanish) sandals

baptism = a religious ceremony that admits a person, especially a baby, to the Christian community

47 **tilts his thumb to his lips** = makes a gesture to show that she has had too many (alcoholic) drinks

saddle shoes =

ON YOUR OWN

Reading

Read pages 35–48 *without stopping.*

Don't try to understand every word—focus on the main ideas.

When you finish, take out your dictionary and use it as you reread these pages. At this time, you can make an entry in your reading journal.

 Increasing Your Reading Speed

To build your reading speed, try this: Begin reading at a certain point and continue for two minutes. Then stop and mark your place. Return to your starting point and read again for two minutes, trying to get past the place you marked. Repeat the process once more.

A Closer Look

And Some More (pages 35–38)

1. Who are the four people who are talking?

2. Someone says, "There's that wide puffy cloud that looks like your face when you wake up after falling asleep with all your clothes on" (36). This statement is:

    _____ a deliberate insult about someone's face.
    _____ an innocent remark that is misunderstood.

3. After reading what the girls say to each other, did you think that was the end of their friendship? Why or why not?

The Family of Little Feet (pages 39–42)

4. How do Esperanza, Lucy, and Rachel feel at first about the high-heeled shoes?

5. How do these people react when they see the girls walking down the street in their high heels?

    Mr. Benny

    the boy on the bicycle

    the group of girls

6. What makes the girls run home fast?

A Rice Sandwich (pages 43–45)

7. Esperanza gives her mother many reasons for eating her lunch at school instead of going home. But what is her real reason for wanting to eat in the canteen?

8. What happens when Esperanza goes to Sister Superior's office?

Chanclas (pages 46–48)

9. Why doesn't Esperanza have any fun at the party at first?

10. What do you think is the most exciting thing for her about that evening?

Write any questions *you* have about this part of the book. Give them to your teacher.

SCENE FROM THE NOVEL

The conversation in "And Some More" can be confusing because sometimes it is impossible to know who is speaking. To understand better what is happening, try creating a script to read aloud.

1. Form a group of four. Each person will take a role and read the part of Esperanza, Nenny, Lucy, or Rachel.

2. Open your books to page 35. Underline the first words spoken in the scene, and write the speaker's name in the margin, like this:

Esperanza <u>The Eskimos got thirty different names for snow,</u> I say. <u>I read it in a book</u>.

3. Continue underlining the words spoken by each character and putting the speaker's name in the margin. The suggestions in the box below may help.

4. Before reading the scene aloud, each of you should practice your part by reading it softly to yourself.

> **Here is one way to interpret the scene:**
>
> Imagine the four girls sitting on Esperanza's front steps. Esperanza points out the type of cloud called "cumulus." Nenny wants to call the clouds by people's names: Nancy, Mildred, Joey, etc. While the other girls go on talking, Nenny gazes up at the clouds and thinks of more names, saying them softly in a sing-song voice. She pays no attention to the other girls.
>
> Meanwhile, Esperanza points out a "wide puffy cloud" that reminds her of how a person's face looks after a nap. Lucy thinks Esperanza is insulting her, so she replies, "Not my face. Looks like your fat face." An argument follows, with Rachel joining in support of her sister.
>
> Esperanza finally says, "That does it!" and standing up angrily, she tells Lucy and Rachel to leave. At first, Rachel says they were only playing, but soon she and Lucy are angrily on their feet, too. Nenny is still sitting

> on the steps, looking up at the sky, talking softly to herself.
>
> When you come to the last four lines of the scene, decide: Are these words part of the conversation or words that pass through Esperanza's mind later? Does Nenny join the conversation at this point? Or has someone else heard the argument and spoken up?

DISCUSSION

1. In "The Family of Little Feet," how are the high-heeled shoes "magic" (40)? How are the shoes "dangerous" (41)?

2. Why do you think Esperanza called the bushel basket "powerful" (42)?

3. As a young girl or boy, did you go to dances? If so, tell how old you were and compare those dances to the party in the church basement where Esperanza danced.

4. How old do you think Esperanza is? Why?

5. If you are keeping a reading journal, share something you have written. Read aloud what you wrote on the left side of the page under "What I Noticed." Then tell why it made an impression on you and what you thought about it.

SUGGESTIONS FOR WRITING

Personal Response

Make an entry in your reading journal. If you like writing poems, think about adding a poem to your journal, a poem that relates to what you have read.

Summarizing

Choose one of the four excerpts from this part of the novel and write a one-paragraph summary. You can begin this way:

In "(title)," Esperanza describes . . .

—an argument with Lucy and Rachel.
—an adventure in ladies' high-heeled shoes.
—a bad experience at school.
—a new experience at a party.

Points of Departure

1. At the baptism party, a boy asks Esperanza to dance, but she is shy and refuses. Later, he watches her dance with her uncle. We can tell it is important to her that this boy is watching her. Do you remember a time when you were younger and you discovered that some boy or girl had noticed you, was interested in you, was watching you? Describe when and where this happened and how it made you feel.

2. Author Sandra Cisneros said,

   > I used to be ashamed to take anyone ... to my house, because if they saw that house they would equate the house with me and my value. And I know that house didn't define me; they just saw the outside. They couldn't see what was inside. (Feroza Jussawalla and Reed Way Dasenbrock, *Interviews with Writers of the Post Colonial World* [Jackson, MS: University Press of Mississippi, 1992], 302)

   On page 5, Esperanza describes how it made her "feel like nothing" when a nun from her school pointed to her apartment and said, "You live *there?*" Then Sister Superior made Esperanza cry by suggesting that she lived in one of the buildings that "even the raggedy men are ashamed to go into" (45).

   What would you say to Esperanza about her feelings of shame? Write her a letter.

3. Imagine that you are Lucy and that you are writing in your diary. Describe the gift of the high-heeled shoes, trying them on, the

reactions of people on the street, and how your sister Rachel almost got into trouble. You have hidden the shoes under a basket on your back porch—will you wear them again?

WORDS TO KNOW

* = irregular verb

PAGE

36   **cute** *(adj.)* Rachel thought the cumulus were **cute**.

puffy *(adj.)* Some clouds look soft and round and **puffy**.

40   **trade** *(v.)* The girls **trade** shoes, exchanging one pair for another.

keep on *(v.)** For a long time, the girls **keep on** trying on the high heels, one pair after another.

scar *(n.)* The girls' legs have many little **scars**.

41   **invisible** *(adj.)* The six cousins in front of the laundromat pretend not to see Esperanza, Lucy, and Rachel. They act as if the three girls were **invisible**.

jealous *(adj.)* Lucy says those girls are **jealous**.

strut *(v.)* Esperanza, Lucy, and Rachel **strut** proudly down the street in their high heels.

dizzy *(adj.)* Rachel seems **dizzy** from the excitement of so many compliments.

44   **appreciate** *(v.)* Esperanza wants her mother to miss her so that her mother will **appreciate** her more.

shy *(adj.)* Esperanza is too **shy** to speak to the nun in the canteen.

45   **faint** *(v.)* Esperanza's mother writes that Esperanza is so skinny she might **faint**.

ashamed *(adj.)* Esperanza thinks anyone would be **ashamed** to live in that row of ugly apartment buildings.

47   **drag** *(v.)* Esperanza, feeling embarrassed, **drags** her heavy feet across the floor.

show off *(v.)** Esperanza's uncle wants to **show off** a new dance that the two of them have learned.

Exercise 1 Write each word next to its definition.

dizzy   jealous   puffy   strut

1. _____ envious, wanting what someone else has

2. _____ walk in a proud, self-satisfied way, showing off

3. _____ feeling confused and off-balance, as if things are going around and around

4. _____ a little swollen

Exercise 2 Use one of the following words or phrases to complete each sentence about the story. You will need to change the forms of three words.

ashamed   cute   drag   keep on   scar   show off

1. Looking up at the fluffy white clouds like balls of cotton, Rachel said that cumulus were _____.

2. The girls wanted to try on all the pairs of shoes, and they _____ passing them around and around, trading one pair for another.

3. There were _____ on the girls legs where they had picked at the scabs on scratches or cuts.

4. Sister Superior upset Esperanza. She pointed to a house that anyone would be _____ of and asked if that were her house. Esperanza was too shy to correct her.

5. Esperanza was ashamed of her old saddle shoes that didn't go with her new dress, so her feet felt heavy and she _____ them across the dance floor.

6. Uncle Nacho wanted to _____ the new dance that he and Esperanza had learned. They danced well together.

Exercise 3   Use the same words to complete these sentences, which are *not* related to the story. You will need to change the form of one word.

ashamed   cute   drag   keep on   scar   show off

1. In the heat of an argument, I said something mean. Afterwards, I felt _____ and asked my friend to forgive me.

2. The box was too heavy to lift, so we had to _____ it across the floor.

3. "_____" is a word used for pretty little things like kittens, puppies, or small children. It's a word more often used by girls and women than by boys or men.

4. I have a _____ on my face where I once got a bad cut.

5. He's a good basketball player, but I don't like having him on my team. All he wants to do is _____.

6. The first time I tried to ride a bike, I couldn't do it. But I _____ trying until I could.

Exercise 4   Draw a line from each word to its opposite.

1. ashamed   a. ugly, unattractive

2. cute   b. full of pride and satisfaction

3. invisible   c. unafraid, confident, bold

4. shy   d. able to be seen

NOUNS	VERBS	ADJECTIVES	ADVERBS
appreciation	appreciate	appreciative	appreciatively

Exercise 5 Look at the chart above for words related to "appreciate." Fill in each blank in the following sentences with the appropriate member of this word family.

1. Esperanza thought that if her mother saw her less, her mother would _____ her more.

2. Maybe if her mother missed her, then when she finally came home, her mother would be more _____ of her.

3. When a friend does something nice for you, what can you do to show your _____?

---

faint

a. *(v.)* to fall unconscious, *(syn.)* to pass out

b. *(adj.)* unclear, weak

c. *(adj.)* dizzy, weak

From *The Newbury House Dictionary of American English*

Exercise 6 Look at the box above. Which meaning does "faint" have in the following sentences? Write the letter of the definition next to each sentence.

_____ 1. The heat in the crowded room made me feel **faint**.

_____ 2. His voice on the telephone was so **faint** that I could hardly hear him.

_____ 3. Is Esperanza really so thin and weak that she might **faint**?

> **trade**
>
> a. (*n.*) commerce in general
>
> b. (*n.*) a type of work, skill
>
> c. (*v.*) to exchange
>
> From *The Newbury House Dictionary of American English*

Exercise 7 Look at the box above. Which meaning does "trade" have in the following sentences? Write the letter of the definition next to each sentence.

_____ 1. He is an electrician who learned his **trade** by working with his father.

_____ 2. The President has appointed her to be the new U.S. **trade** representative in Europe.

_____ 3. The girls took turns with the different pairs of shoes, **trading** one pair for another.

⁓ Part Five ⁓

Hips
The First Job
Papa Who Wakes Up Tired in the Dark
Born Bad
Elenita, Cards, Palm, Water
(pages 49–64)

". . . a dusty Palm Sunday cross. . ." (63)

BEFORE YOU READ

PAGE

49 **I like coffee, I like tea . . .** (This is part of a rhyme that girls chant while jumping rope.)

50 **She is stupid alright** = I agree that she is stupid

Bones got to give. = Bones have got to give way, to move under pressure.

to lullaby it = to sing the baby to sleep

double-dutch = a jump rope game in which two people stand facing each other and holding the ends of two long ropes; each person circles their arms in opposite directions so that the ropes pass over and under the jumper(s) in the middle

practice shaking it = try moving her hips quickly

51 **merengue** = (Spanish) a dance from the Caribbean

tembleque = (Spanish) a soft dessert that quivers or shakes when touched

not a girl, not a boy, . . . = (This is part of an old jump rope rhyme:

> Fudge, fudge,
> Call the judge,
> Mama's got a newborn baby.
> It's not a girl, it's not a boy,
> It's just an ordinary baby.)

52 **First Holy Communion** = a sacrament in the Catholic Church for children around age seven

she doesn't get it or won't = she doesn't understand or refuses to

	I can tell = I know (from Lucy and Rachel's facial expressions or gestures)	
53	**my social security number** = a nine-digit identification number given by the government to each worker in the U.S.	
	the dime store = a store with a variety of inexpensive goods	
54	**break time** = a short rest period for employees	
	punched the time clock = put their work cards into a machine to record what time they arrived	
	Oriental (Many people now prefer the word "Asian.")	
56	**abuelito** = (Spanish) an affectionate word for "grandfather"	
	Está muerto = (Spanish) He's dead.	
58	**Joan Crawford** = Hollywood movie star of the 1940's	
59	**step stool** = a short ladder with one or two flat steps and a seat on top	
62	**the planets were all mixed up yesterday** (Elenita believes in astrology; she thinks the positions and movements of the planets influence people's lives.)	
63	**a plaster saint and a dusty Palm Sunday cross** = symbols of Catholicism	
	the voodoo hand = symbol of a Caribbean religious cult	
	these cards = Tarot cards, used to predict the future	
	los espíritus = (Spanish) the spirits of dead people	

ON YOUR OWN

Reading

Read pages 49–64 without *stopping*.

Don't try to understand every word—focus on the main ideas.

When you finish, take out your dictionary and use it when necessary as you reread these pages.

A Closer Look

Hips (pages 49–52)

1. According to the girls, what are two things that hips are good for?

2. What are Rachel, Lucy, and Esperanza doing differently from Nenny when they take their turns at jumping rope?

The First Job (pages 53–55)

3. Why does Esperanza need money?

4. What do you think Esperanza should have done after the man kissed her?

　　_____ Run home and refused to go back to work there.
　　_____ Reported the man to the boss.
　　_____ Stayed out of the coatroom and avoided that man.
　　_____ Other: _____

Papa Who Wakes Up Tired in the Dark (pages 56–57)

5. Write a question about Esperanza's father to ask your classmates. It can be a question that asks for information (see pages 56–57) or a question that requires readers to use their imaginations.

Born Bad (pages 58–61)

6. What does Esperanza feel guilty about?

7. What secret did Esperanza share with her Aunt Lupe?

Elenita, Cards, Palm, Water **(pages 62–64)**

8. What in particular did Esperanza go to the fortune teller to find out about?

9. Have you ever had your fortune told? If so, describe the experience.

Write any questions *you* have about this part of the novel.

DISCUSSION

1. What does Esperanza mean when she says Nenny "is in a world we don't belong to anymore" (52)?

2. Esperanza goes to a private school. Her father thinks children who go to public school "turn out bad" (53). Do you agree with his opinion of public schools? Why or why not?

3. What should Esperanza have done after the man kissed her? Compare and explain your answers to question 4 on page 79.

4. Ask each other the questions you wrote about Esperanza's father (from question 5 on page 79.)

5. Page 61: Explain what Aunt Lupe means when she tells Esperanza to keep writing because it will keep her free.

6. To try to see into the future, Elenita uses Tarot cards, palm-reading, and a mug of water. People try to predict the future in many ways; make a list of some ways you have heard of.

7. Have each person in your group take a piece of paper and write their name at the top. Pass the papers. When you receive someone's paper, write on it a prediction (a good one!) about that person's future, and then pass the paper to someone else. You can write realistic predictions using what you know about your classmates or fantastic ones using your imagination. When there are several predictions on each person's paper, give them back and enjoy reading them.

SUGGESTIONS FOR WRITING

Personal Response

Make an entry in your reading journal.

Your journal can be a source of ideas for essays about the novel. Looking back through your journal entries, you might find something you have written a little about that you would like to expand on, or you might find recurring themes (ideas that come up repeatedly) that you want to write about.

Summarizing

Write a summary of "The First Job." You can begin,

When Esperanza needed to get a job to help pay for school, her Aunt Lupe found her one.

Your summary should include the answers to the following questions:

Where was the job?
Why did she have to lie?
What did she have to do on the job?
Was the work hard?
Where did she go during her break?
Who did she meet there?
What was the man like at first?
Then what happened?

Points of Departure

1. Your first job: Are you working there now, or was it 30 years ago? Or is your first job still in your future? Describe the job and your feelings about it.

2. Esperanza tells us a little about what will happen when her father returns to Mexico after the death of his father. She mentions a "tomb with flowers shaped like spears in a white vase because this is how they send the dead away in that country" (56).

    How do people "send the dead away" in your culture? Are there customs that involve clothing, food, flowers, music, taking care of the body, bringing people together? Explain what people traditionally do when someone dies.

3. What do you think the sky represents for Esperanza? Reread page 33 and the poem on pages 60–61. Also, recall her description of herself as "a balloon tied to an anchor" (9). Explain what you think the sky means for Esperanza, using quotations from the book to illustrate and support your ideas.

WORDS TO KNOW

* = irregular verb

PAGE

49   **turn into** *(v.)* Nenny says a girl might **turn into** a man if she doesn't develop hips.

50   **make fun of** *(v.)** Esperanza doesn't want Lucy or Rachel to **make fun of** Nenny.

  authority *(n.)* Esperanza speaks with **authority** when she talks about hips because she has information from Alicia.

spread *(v.)** Rachel warns that if a woman has too many babies, her "behind will **spread**."

make (something) up *(v.)** When Esperanza gives advice about hips, she is just **making it up** as she speaks.

52 **disgusted** *(adj.)* Esperanza can see that Lucy and Rachel are **disgusted** with Nenny, even though they don't say they are.

54 **show up** *(v.)** Eperanza's aunt told her to **show up** at the Peter Pan Photo Finishers the next day.

lie *(v.)* Esperanza **lied** about her age. She said she was older than she really was.

shift *(n.)* The workers punched the time clock at the start of each **shift**.

56 **crumple** *(v.)* Eperanza's father "**crumples** like a coat and cries" when he tells her his father is dead.

58 **evil** *(adj.)* Esperanza's mother says Esperanza was born on an **evil** day because of what she and her friends did to Aunt Lupe.

disease *(n.)* Aunt Lupe suffered from a terrible **disease**.

limp *(adj.)* Aunt Lupe's bones lost their strength and became "**limp** as worms."

59 **imitate** *(v.)* In their game, the girls would **imitate** other people's ways of talking and acting.

63 **palm** *(n.)* Elenita takes Esperanza's hand and looks into her **palm** to see her future.

64 **hug** *(v.)* Elenita hits her children for fighting and then **hugs** them.

Exercise 1 Write each word next to its definition.

authority   a disease   evil   palm

1. _____ very bad, wicked, harmful

2. _____ power to influence because of special knowledge or experience

3. _____ the inner surface of the hand from the base of the fingers to the wrist

4. _____ a disorder causing serious illness or sickness

Exercise 2 Use one of the following words or phrases to complete each sentence about the story. You will need to change two word forms.

**crumple   make fun of   make up   show up
spread   turn into**

1. Nenny thought a girl might _____ a man if she didn't develop hips.

2. Esperanza spoke quickly so that Rachel and Lucy wouldn't _____ her sister.

3. Although Esperanza talked as if she had real knowledge about hips, she was just _____ it _____ as she spoke.

4. Rachel warned the others not to have too many babies or they'd get fat. "Your behind will _____," she said.

5. Esperanza did not have to make an appointment for an interview at the photo finishers. Her aunt told her to just _____.

6. Esperanza's Papa came into her room early one morning, sat on her bed, and told her his father had died. Then he couldn't hold back his feelings and he _____ "like a coat."

Exercise 3 Use the same words to complete the following sentences, which are *not* related to the story. Change word forms as needed.

crumple   make fun of   make up   show up
spread   turn into

1. I would feel embarrassed if someone _____ my clothes.

2. AIDS is a terrible disease that has _____ to many parts of the world.

3. My friend was supposed to meet me at 7:00, but he was late. He finally _____ at 7:30.

4. Monarch caterpillars _____ beautiful orange and black butterflies.

5. The teacher asked us to write a story. It couldn't be about something that had really happened; we had to _____ a story.

6. My first try at writing a story was terrible, so I _____ up the paper and threw it in the wastebasket.

> The adjectives "disgust**ed**" vs. "disgust**ing**":
>
> Someone will feel disgust**ed** if something or someone is disgust**ing**. For example,
>
> He chews his food with his mouth open. It's **disgusting**.
>
> I was **disgusted** by the way that he ate.
>
> We were **disgusted** with the way she spoke so rudely to her secretary.
>
> We thought her behavior was **disgusting**.

NOUNS	VERBS	ADJECTIVES	ADVERBS
_____	_____	disgusted disgusting	

Exercise 4 Read the information in the box about "disgusted" and "disgusting." Use your dictionary to complete the chart above. Then fill in each blank in the sentences below with the appropriate member of this word family.

1. Esperanza could see expressions of _____ on Rachel and Lucy's faces.

2. It was Nenny's childishness that _____ them.

3. Rachel and Lucy were _____ with Nenny, but they didn't say anything.

Exercise 5 Which three words or phrases are possible in the sentence below? Circle them.

      evil   **hug**   **imitate**   **lie**   **make fun of**   **turn into**

You can _____ another person.

Exercise 6 Is the underlined word in each sentence a *noun, verb,* or *adjective?*

_____ 1. Esperanza told a lie.

_____ 2. Her aunt told her to lie about her age.

_____ 3. Elenita got up to hit and hug her children.

_____ 4. She gave her children a hug.

_____ 5. Esperanza says "there was no evil" in her aunt's birth.

_____ 6. Do you believe Esperanza was born on an evil day?

---

shift

a. *(v.)* to change from one position to another

b. *(n.)* a change of ideas

c. *(n.)* a segment of work time

From *The Newbury House Dictionary of American English*

Exercise 7 Look at the box above. Which meaning does "shift" have in the following sentences? Write the letter of the definition next to each sentence.

_____ 1. The people waiting in line stood **shifting** their weight from one foot to the other.

_____ 2. My **shift** at the hospital runs from 7:00 A.M. to 3:00 P.M.

_____ 3. Since the election, there has been a **shift** in public opinion.

> **limp**
>
> a. *(n.)* an uneven walk as from an injury to the leg or foot
>
> b. *(v.)* to walk with a limp, *(syn.)* to hobble
>
> c. *(adj.)* lacking firmness or stiffness
>
> From *The Newbury House Dictionary of American English*

Exercise 8 Look at the box above. Which meaning does "limp" have in each of these sentences? Write the letter of the definition next to each sentence.

_____ 1. Someone whose foot is hurt might **limp** when walking.

_____ 2. After spraining my ankle, I walked with a **limp**.

_____ 3. Aunt Lupe's legs became **limp** because of the disease, so she could not stand up.

TEST YOURSELF

VOCABULARY REVIEW FOR PARTS 3 AND 4

1. Are the meanings of the underlined words similar or different? Write "similar" or "different" in the space next to each pair.

   _____ **a.** The scar was almost <u>invisible</u>.

   The scar was almost <u>impossible to see</u>.

   _____ **b.** The test was <u>simple</u>.

   The test was <u>tough</u>.

   _____ **c.** They're <u>jealous</u> of your success.

   They're <u>envious</u> of your success.

   _____ **d.** The plane <u>took off</u> late.

   The plane <u>landed</u> late.

   _____ **e.** Two men <u>traded</u> seats.

   Two men <u>exchanged</u> seats.

   _____ **f.** Her earrings <u>dangle</u>.

   Her earrings <u>hang down and swing loosely</u>.

   _____ **g.** Will he <u>keep on</u> smoking?

   Will he <u>give up</u> smoking?

2. Choose the phrase from the list below that best completes each sentence about the story.

> . . . **imagine** seeing mice.
>
> . . . **get to** wear nice clothes.
>
> . . . **show off** their new dance.
>
> . . . **strut** down the street together.
>
> . . . **drag** her heavy feet across the floor.

a. Marin wanted a job where she would _____

b. Alicia knew that she didn't _____

c. Wearing high heels, the girls tried to _____

d. At the dance, Esperanza had to _____

e. Uncle Nacho and Esperanza got to _____

3. Answer the following questions about the story. Was it Esperanza, Esperanza's mother, Marin, or the Vargas children?

a. Who dared to look at boys without **blinking**? _____

b. Who did Esperanza want to **appreciate** her more? _____

c. Who wrote that she hoped Esperanza would not **faint**? _____

d. Who was too **shy** to speak? _____

e. Who **didn't know any better than** to play on the roof? _____

4. Use the clues given below to fill in the words in the puzzle.

ACROSS
1. a little swollen
4. working or moving by itself without direct human control
6. little and pretty
8. something seen that is not clear or sharp
9. sensible, with good judgment
10. off-balance and confused

DOWN
2. mistake, imperfection, offense
3. saliva
5. feeling guilty or embarrassed
7. narrow street between or behind city buildings

All the words in the puzzle appear in this list:

alley	automatic	cute	fault	scar
appreciate	blink	dizzy	invisible	spit
ashamed	blur	drag	puffy	wise

The House on Mango Street **91**

Part Six

Geraldo No Last Name
Edna's Ruthie
The Earl of Tennessee
Sire
Four Skinny Trees
(pages 65–75)

"Earl is a jukebox repairman" (71).

BEFORE YOU READ

PAGE

65   **hit and run** = an accident in which a car hits a person or another car and the driver speeds away without stopping

cumbias and salsas and rancheras = kinds of Latin American dances

66   **an intern** = a doctor-in-training

brazer = (Spanish: bracero) a Mexican who comes to the U.S. to work

wet-back = (pejorative) an illegal immigrant from Mexico

money orders = checks bought at a bank or post office as a safe way of sending money through the mail

67   **babushka** – a head scarf

threw out = forced to move out of a rented room or apartment

the Emperor's nightingale = a bird with a very beautiful song, from a story by Hans Christian Andersen

69   **braille** = system of raised dots on paper for blind people to read with their fingertips

"The Walrus and the Carpenter" = a poem by Lewis Carroll, author of *Alice in Wonderland*

71   **The word is** = People say

73   **a punk** = (pejorative) a rebellious teenaged boy who tends to get into trouble

ON YOUR OWN

Reading

Read pages 65–75 *without stopping*.

Don't try to understand every word—focus on the main ideas.

When you finish, take out your dictionary and use it as necessary while you reread these pages.

A Closer Look

Geraldo No Last Name (pages 65–66)

1. Where did Marin meet Geraldo?

2. How did Geraldo die?

3. What does Esperanza mean when she says, ". . . if the surgeon had only come, they would know who to notify and where" (66)?

4. Do you know anyone who, like Geraldo, went to another country to earn money to send home? If so, write about this person.

Edna's Ruthie (pages 67–69)

5. What do you notice about Ruthie that is unusual?

The Earl of Tennessee (pages 70–71)

6. According to the neighbors, who sometimes comes to Earl's apartment?

7. Do you think the neighbors are right? Why or why not?

Sire (pages 72–73)

8. Why does Esperanza say, "I had to look back hard, just once, like he [Sire] was glass" (72)?

9. What does Esperanza think about as she leans out her window in the evening and talks to the trees?

Four Skinny Trees (pages 74–75)

10. What is it about the four skinny elm trees that attracts Esperanza?

Write any question *you* have about this part of the book.

DISCUSSION

1. How do you think Marin felt about Geraldo's death? Give reasons for your answers.

2. Esperanza writes, "They never knew about the two-room flats and sleeping rooms he [Geraldo] rented, the weekly money orders sent home, the currency exchange" (66). Who does she mean by "they"—who is it that doesn't understand the life of someone like Geraldo?

3. What differences do you see between Esperanza and Sire's girlfriend, Lois?

4. What do you think goes through Sire's mind when he looks at Esperanza?

5. Esperanza says the four skinny trees understand her and she understands them. What similarities can you see between her and the trees? Fill in the table that follows on page 98.

THE TREES	ESPERANZA
"four skinny trees"	Esperanza says she has a skinny neck and pointy elbows.
They "do not belong here."	
"Their strength is secret."	
"Four who grew despite concrete."	

SUGGESTIONS FOR WRITING

Personal Response

Make an entry in your reading journal.

Summarizing

Write a one-paragraph summary of "Four Skinny Trees." To get started, try rereading the story and writing down key words and ideas. Then close your book and write the summary from your notes.

Points of Departure

1. Imagine that you are Geraldo. It's Saturday afternoon, and you are lying on your bed, listening to the radio, thinking of home. You decide to write a letter to send with this week's money order. Who is the letter for? What will it say about your life in the U.S., and about your thoughts of home? Write the letter.

2. Imagine that you are Marin and you are writing a letter to your friend Angelina in Puerto Rico. It is the day after the death of Geraldo, and you want to tell her about him. Describe what happened and how you feel about it.

3. Esperanza's mother tells her not to talk to Sire, whom her father calls "a punk." How much should parents control the friendships their daughters have with boys? How much freedom should they give their daughters?

   What about sons? How much should parents control their sons' friendships with girls, and how much freedom should sons be given? Should the rules for sons and daughters be the same or different? Explain your reasons for your answers.

4. Create a short poem by borrowing phrases from the novel, as described on page 47 in the *Companion*. Focus on a character: Geraldo, Ruthie, Sire, Lois, or Esperanza. Choose a title for your poem.

   If you prefer, you could write a poem that is completely original. You might like to choose a word or phrase from the novel as the starting point for your poem.

WORDS TO KNOW

* = irregular verb

PAGE

66   **shame** *(n.)* Geraldo's death was a terrible **shame**.

       surgeon *(n.)* Geraldo needed a **surgeon**, but there was only an intern on duty in the emergency room.

       notify *(v.)* No one knew who to **notify** about Geraldo's death.

shrug *(v.)* Esperanza imagines Geraldo's friends **shrugging** their shoulders, as if to say, "I guess we'll never know."

68   **deal** *(v.)** When the children played cards that night, they let Ruthie **deal**.

70   **sigh** *(n.)* The door to Earl's apartment seems to open with a **sigh**.

mold *(n.)* Earl's basement apartment smells of **mold**.

71   **leap** *(v.)* Earl's two little black dogs **leap** and curl in the air "like an apostrophe and comma."

72   **prove** *(v.)** Esperanza wanted to **prove** to herself that she wasn't scared by Sire's looking at her.

73   **grip** *(n.)* Esperanza dreamed she felt the **grip** of a boy's arms holding her close.

74   **belong** *(v.)* The four little elm trees seem out of place on Mango Street. They do not **belong** there.

ferocious *(adj.)* The four skinny trees send down **ferocious** roots to grip the earth.

droop *(v.)* Esperanza imagines the four trees all **drooping** "like tulips in a glass."

concrete *(n.)* The **concrete** surrounding the trees has not kept them from growing.

Exercise 1 Write each word next to its definition.

concrete   a grip   a sigh   a surgeon

1. _____ a very firm forceful hold on someone or something

2. _____ a sound of breath let out that expresses tiredness, sadness, or pleasure

3. _____ a mixture of cement, sand, and gravel used for buildings, roads, sidewalks, and so on

4. _____ a doctor who specializes in performing operations

Exercise 2 Use one of the following words to complete each sentence about the story. Change word forms as needed.

belong   droop   leap   notify   prove   shrug

1. Geraldo was carrying no identification papers, so no one could _____ his family of his death.

2. Esperanza imagined Geraldo's friends back home wondering what had happened to him. She thought they would just _____, as if to say, "Who knows?"

3. When Earl's two little black dogs would _____, their bodies would curl "like an apostrophe and comma."

4. Esperanza wanted to _____ to herself that she wasn't afraid to look back at Sire when he was looking at her.

5. The four skinny elm trees do not _____ in the city, surrounded by concrete. They are out of place.

6. The trees have managed to grow despite their surroundings. Esperanza imagines that if one grew discouraged, all four would _____, their branches hanging down.

Exercise 3 Use the same words to complete the following sentences, which are *not* related to the story. Change word forms as needed.

belong   droop   leap   notify   prove   shrug

1. In court, a prosecutor tries to _____ that a person accused of a crime is guilty.

2. The landlord _____ the tenants that their rent was going to be raised.

3. When the woman asked her husband what he would like to have for dinner, he gave a _____ and said, "I don't care."

4. The students were tired at the end of the day, and their heads _____ as they sat at their desks.

5. I was offered a wonderful new job, so of course I _____ at the chance and said, "Yes, I'll take it!"

6. Sometimes a family buys a house that they used to rent. Then the house _____ to them.

Exercise 4 Where would you find the following?

          a surgeon   concrete   mold   ferocious animals

1. _____ in the jungle

2. _____ in a hospital

3. _____ in a dark, damp place

4. _____ in buildings and sidewalks

---

deal

a. *(v.)** to give, esp. cards to players of a card game

b. *(v.)** **to deal in:** to buy [something] from producers and sell it to customers

c. *(v.)** **to deal with**: to treat, to manage

d. *(v.)** **to deal with**: to concern, to be about

From *The Newbury House Dictionary of American English*

Exercise 5 Look at the box above. Which meaning does "deal" have in the following sentences? Write the letter of the definition next to each sentence.

_____ 1. The owner of the junk store **deals** in used furniture.

_____ 2. The girls let Ruthie **deal** when they played cards.

_____ 3. *The House on Mango Street* **deals** with the experiences of a young girl growing up.

_____ 4. What do you think of the way Alicia's father **has dealt** with her fear of mice?

> **shame**
>
> a. *(n.)* a sad situation, a pity
>
> b. *(n.)* a sad feeling of knowing one has done wrong
>
> c. *(v.)* to cause [someone] to feel bad through guilt
>
> From *The Newbury House Dictionary of American English*

Exercise 6 Look at the box above. Which meaning does "shame" have in the following sentences? Write the letter of the definition next to each sentence.

_____ 1. Do you think Esperanza **shamed** her parents by imitating her sick Aunt Lupe?

_____ 2. Esperanza felt a painful sense of **shame** when the nun pointed at her family's poor apartment on Loomis Street.

_____ 3. Geraldo shouldn't have died; his death was a terrible **shame**.

Part Seven

No Speak English
Rafaela Who Drinks Coconut & Papaya Juice on Tuesdays
Sally
Minerva Writes Poems
Bums in the Attic
(pages 76–87)

"... he plays dominoes" (79).

BEFORE YOU READ

PAGE

76   **Mamacita** = (appreciative) little Mama

       Mamasota = (pejorative) big Mama

77   **Holy smokes** = an expression of surprise

78   **Cuándo?** = (Spanish) When?

79   **Rapunzel** = a princess in a fairy tale who was imprisoned in a tower with no door, but a prince climbed up her long hair and in through the window

81   **Cleopatra** = an Egyptian queen famous for her beauty

82   **the muddy cake** = dark makeup for outlining the eyes

85   **lets him know enough is enough** = tells him she will not tolerate any more

       Same story. = The same thing happens again.

       she comes over black and blue = she comes to Esperanza's house covered with bruises

ON YOUR OWN

Reading

Read pages 76–87 *without stopping.*

A Closer Look

No Speak English (pages 76–78)

1. Complete these sentences:

   When Mamacita says "No speak English" to someone at the door, she means, "_____."

   When she says these same words to her little boy, she means, "_____."

2. Why does it break Mamacita's heart to hear her son sing the Pepsi commercial?

Rafaela Who Drinks Coconut & Papaya Juice on Tuesdays (pages 79–80)

3. Write a question to ask your classmates about Rafaela. It can be a question that asks for information (see pages 79–80) or a question that asks for an opinion about her. Then write your own answer to your question.

Sally (pages 81–83)

4. What does Sally's father mean when he says that "to be this beautiful is trouble"?

5. How does Sally change after school?

6. Practice reading aloud the last paragraph of "Sally."

Minerva Writes Poems (pages 84–85)

7. What do Esperanza and Minerva have in common?

8. How does Esperanza feel about Minerva's situation?

Bums in the Attic (pages 86–87)

9. Where does Esperanza's family go on Sundays? Why do they go there?

10. What is your opinion of Esperanza's plan to invite bums to stay upstairs in her attic?

Write any questions *you* have about this part of the book.

DISCUSSION

1. Do you feel more sympathy for Mamacita or for her husband? Explain your answers.

2. Discuss the questions each of you wrote about Rafaela (from question 3 on page 107).

3. Take turns and read aloud the last paragraph of "Sally" (pages 82–83). In this paragraph, is Esperanza talking about Sally's dreams and worries or her own? Explain your answers.

4. When Minerva, beaten black and blue by her husband, comes over to Esperanza's house, she asks what she can do. How would you answer her question?

5. One person in the group takes the role of Esperanza. The others in the group take the roles of other characters. Esperanza explains why she would invite bums to stay in her attic, and the other characters tell her what they think of her plan and why.

SUGGESTIONS FOR WRITING

Personal Response

Make an entry in your reading journal.

Summarizing

Write a one-paragraph summary of "Mamacita" or "Minerva Writes Poems."

Points of Departure

1. With a partner or on your own, write a conversation between two characters who have appeared so far in the novel. For example, you could write:

   - A conversation between Marin and Geraldo at the dance, or
   - A telephone conversation between Mamacita and her husband before she came to the United States, or
   - A conversation between Rafaela and her husband when he comes home from playing dominoes.

   When you have written a draft, read your conversation aloud with a partner.

2. In an interview, Sandra Cisnernos spoke about "No Speak English" and the fear of English felt by some immigrants to the U.S.:

   > I just wanted to talk there about peoples' fear of the English language and also why they want to keep their own language. The language, for a lot of people, was a link back; it meant that you were going to get back eventually. That's why some people refused to learn English because they were assuming, as so many immigrants did, that there was a road back. And it's a frightening thing when you let go of a language because you've let go your tiny thin string back home . . . (Jussawalla and Dasenbrock, *Interviews with Writers*, 294)

Have you ever felt this fear of English, or do you know someone who has it? Describe this fear and its effect on people's lives. You can write about your own experiences or those of people you know.

3. Mamacita sits at the window and sighs for the pink house she left behind. Have you ever felt homesick? Describe when and where you felt this way. What did you miss most about your home? Did your feelings change over time? Write about how you experienced homesickness.

4. Much of what we learn about relationships comes from observing people around us. What do you think Esperanza is learning about marriage from observing the husbands and wives that she knows? Think about her great-grandparents, Mamacita, Rafaela, and Minerva. Tell what impression of marriage you think Esperanza has and why. Do you feel this is a true picture of what marriage is? Explain your answer.

WORDS TO KNOW

* = irregular verb

PAGE

76   **mean** *(adj.)* Esperanza thinks it is **mean** to call Mamacita "Mamasota."

78   **hysterical** *(adj.)* Mamacita sometimes cries out in a high, **hysterical** voice.

80   **bitter** *(adj.)* Rafaela wishes for drinks as sweet as the island she comes from, "not **bitter** like an empty room."

81   **strict** *(adj.)* Sally's father belongs to a very **strict** religion.

dip *(v.)* Esperanza imagines **dipping** a little brush into a cake of dark eyeliner and painting her eyes like Sally's.

82   **mood** *(n.)* Esperanza will wait until her mother is in a good **mood** before she asks to buy nylons like Sally's.

bleed *(v.)** Sally and her friend Cheryl had a fight, and Sally made Cheryl's ear **bleed**.

lean *(v.)* Sally **leans** against the schoolyard fence alone now.

83   **nosy** *(adj.)* Esperanza imagines a place free from **nosy** neighbors.

84   **raise** *(v.)* Minerva's mother **raised** her kids alone, and it seems her daughters will be single mothers, too.

fold *(v.)* Minerva writes her poems on little pieces of paper, then **folds** them again and again.

85   **be through (with)** Minerva tells her husband that she **is through** and wants no more of him.

86   **stare** *(v.)* Esperanza is ashamed of the way her family **stares** at the houses and gardens of the rich.

Exercise 1 Write each adjective next to its definition.

        hysterical   **mean**   **nosy**   **strict**

1. _____ unkind, not nice to others

2. _____ in a state of uncontrollable crying or laughing

3. _____ severe, demanding

4. _____ too interested in other people's concerns

Exercise 2 Use one of the following words or phrases to complete each sentence about the story. Changes word forms as needed.

      be through   **dip**   **fold**   **lean**   **mood**   **stare**

1. Esperanza wanted Sally to teach her how to _____ a little brush into makeup and paint dark lines around her eyes, like Cleopatra.

2. One day, after her next birthday, when her mother was in a good _____, Esperanza planned ask permission to start wearing nylons.

3. Sally lost her friend and no longer had anyone to _____ against the schoolyard fence with her.

4. Minerva would write poems on little pieces of paper and then _____ them again and again until they were tiny.

5. One day Minerva told her abusive husband to leave. She said that they _____ and made him move out.

6. Esperanza was ashamed of the way her family _____ out the windows of their car at the houses of rich people.

Exercise 3 Now use the same words to complete the following sentences, which are *not* related to the story. Change word forms as needed.

       be through   dip   fold   lean   mood   stare

1. When I'm in a bad _____, I don't want to talk to anyone.

2. Does it make you feel uncomfortable if people _____ at you?

3. Signs on the subway warn people not to _____ against the doors.

4. I _____ my toes into the water to see how cold the pool was.

5. The teacher said that as soon as the students _____ with the test, they could leave.

6. I took the clean towels out of the laundry basket, _____ them neatly, and put them away.

NOUNS	VERBS	ADJECTIVES	ADVERBS
blood	bleed*	bloody	

Exercise 4 Look at the chart above for words related to "bleed." Fill in each blank in the following sentences with the appropriate member of this word family.

1. Sally gave Cheryl a _____ ear.

2. Cheryl's ear _____ because of something Sally did.

3. When Cheryl bit Sally, was there any _____?

114 The ESL Reader's Companion

> **raise**
>
> a. *(v.)* to lift up, *(syn.)* to elevate
>
> b. *(v.)* to help a child to grow up
>
> c. *(n.)* an increase in salary
>
> From *The Newbury House Dictionary of American English*

Exercise 5 Look at the box above. Which meaning does "raise" have in the following sentences? Write the letter of the definition next to each sentence.

_____ 1. I did such a good job that the boss is giving me a **raise.**

_____ 2. Do you **raise** your hand in class when you have something to say?

_____ 3. Minerva's mother **raised** her children alone, as a single parent.

> **bitter**
>
> a. *(adj.)* having a sharp, acid taste
>
> b. *(adj.)* giving pain, hurtful
>
> c. *(adj.)* angry, hateful
>
> From *The Newbury House Dictionary of American English*

Exercise 6 Look at the box above. Which meaning does "bitter" have in the following sentences? Write the letter of the definition next to each sentence.

_____ 1. Leaving her home to live in the U.S. has been a **bitter** experience for Mamacita.

_____ 2. Rafaela likes sweet drinks, not **bitter** ones.

_____ 3. Do you think Rafaela feels **bitter** about being locked in by her husband?

TEST YOURSELF

VOCABULARY REVIEW FOR PARTS 5 AND 6

1. Which one of the three choices is *impossible*? Cross it out.

a. You might **hug** . . .   your mother / a child / a disease.

b. You could **crumple** . . .   a dollar / a rock / a newspaper.

c. You might **belong to** . . .   a team / a club / a car.

d. You could **grip** . . .   my hand / your education / your wallet.

e. You might **leap** . . .   a lake / a puddle / a fence.

2. Answer the following questions about the story. Was it Esperanza, Lucy, Rachel, Aunt Lupe, Geraldo, or Elenita?

a. Who spoke as if she were an **authority** on hips? _____

b. Who did Esperanza think might **make fun of** Nenny? _____

c. Who **made up** their own jump rope songs? _____

d. Who lay in bed, her bones "**limp** as worms"? _____

e. Who read Esperanza's **palm**? _____

f. Who needed a **surgeon**? _____

3. Which four words could you use in the sentence below? Circle them.

    disgusted   lied   notified   shrugged   sighed
    hugged   proved   shamed   showed up

    Esperanza _____ .

4. Find and circle the words defined below. Words are written going down, across from left to right, or diagonally from left to right. Write each word next to its definition.

```
C X S P R E A D F
M O L D K P K R E
W N N K X R Z O R
H W P C H O B O O
B S X G R V L P C
T H Z M V E W W I
R I M I T A T E O
Z F E V I L X E U
R T Q D E A L L S
```

a. _ _ _ _ = to give out cards to each player in a card game

b. _ _ _ _ = very bad, wicked, harmful

c. _ _ _ _ = a dark greenish substance that grows in warm damp places

d. _ _ _ _ _ = to hang or bend down as if tired or weak

e. _ _ _ _ _ = to show to be true, give proof of

f. _ _ _ _ _ = a period of working time in a factory, etc. (or the people who work during it)

g. _ _ _ _ _ _ = to become longer or wider, to cover a large area

h. _ _ _ _ _ _ _ = to copy someone's way of talking, behaving, or moving

i. _ _ _ _ _ _ _ _ = a mixture of cement, sand, and gravel used for buildings, roads, sidewalks, and so on

j. _ _ _ _ _ _ _ _ _ = very fierce, savage

Part Eight

Beautiful & Cruel
A Smart Cookie
What Sally Said
The Monkey Garden
Red Clowns
(pages 88–100)

"I was standing by the tilt-a-whirl . . ." (99)

BEFORE YOU READ

PAGE

88   **the ball and chain** = the heavy iron ball and chain that keep a prisoner from escaping

90   **a smart cookie** = an intelligent girl

        I could've been somebody = I could have become an important, successful person (but I didn't)

91   **Madame Butterfly** = a character in an Italian opera who kills herself after the lover who left her returns only to take away their son

        comadres = (Spanish) best friends and godmothers to each others' children

92   **lard** = pig fat used in cooking

95   **pickup** = a kind of truck

        Rip Van Winkle = a man who fell asleep in the woods and slept for 20 years, from a story by Washington Irving

96   **buddies** = friends

97   **how come I felt** = why did I feel

ON YOUR OWN

Reading

Read pages 88–100 without stopping.

A Closer Look

Beautiful & Cruel (pages 88–89)

1. Esperanza says it's easy for Nenny to talk with confidence about the future because Nenny is pretty. Which gives a person a greater advantage in life: being good-looking or being smart? Why?

2. On page 88, who are "the others who lay their necks on the threshold waiting for the ball and chain"? What—or who—is the ball and chain?

3. Who is "beautiful and cruel"? How is she cruel?

4. Do you think Esperanza looks forward to growing up and getting married? Why or why not?

A Smart Cookie (pages 90–91)

5. How does Esperanza's mother feel now about the fact that she quit school? Why does she feel this way?

What Sally Said (pages 92–93)

6. Sally says her father never hits her hard. Do you believe her?

7. Why do you think Sally says this?

8. What is your opinion of Sally's mother? Give reasons for your opinion.

The Monkey Garden (pages 94–98)

9. The description of the garden (pages 94–95) is rich in details that appeal to the five senses. Which details do you like best? Give an example of at least one detail from the story for each sense:

   smell

   hearing

   taste

   touch

   sight

10. What does Esperanza get angry about?

11. What happens after Esperanza confronts the boys?

Red Clowns (pages 99–100)

12. Where does this incident take place?

13. What do you think happened to Esperanza?

Write any questions *you* have about this part of the book.

DISCUSSION

1. Compare your answers to question 1 on page 121 about the advantages of good looks and intelligence. Give reasons for your answers.

2. On page 89, what does Esperanza mean when she says she has begun a quiet war? What is she fighting for?

3. Do you think Esperanza was right to be upset about Sally and Tito and his friends? Why or why not?

4. What do you think would have happened if Esperanza had run to her own mother instead of to Tito's?

5. On page 99, why does Esperanza say that Sally lied?

6. Esperanza's mother fantasizes about being a famous opera singer. Do you ever fantasize about being famous? Have each person in your group take a slip of paper and complete the sentence,

> I like to imagine myself as a famous _____ because then I could . . .

Drop the slips of paper into a bag and mix them up. Take turns drawing them out one by one and reading them aloud.

SUGGESTIONS FOR WRITING

Personal Response

Make an entry in your reading journal.

Summarizing

Activity 1 Read the following summary of "A Smart Cookie."

Summary A "A Smart Cookie" describes Esperanza's mother as a smart and talented woman who doesn't have a good job or good opportunities in life because she has little education. She quit school because she was ashamed of her clothes, and now she regrets that and tells her daughter to study hard.

Read summaries B and C, and think about why they are not as good as summary A.

Summary B Esperanza's mother isn't happy with her life. She doesn't get to do things that she would like to do. I think that when people get older, they see things differently from the way they saw them when they were young. I guess Esperanza's mother made a bad choice when she was a girl, and now she knows it.

Summary C In "A Smart Cookie," Esperanza's mother says, "I could've been somebody." She can sing an opera and fix a TV. One time she sings Madame Butterfly while cooking oatmeal. She tells Esperanza to go to school, and she says, "Got to take care all your own." She quit school because of her clothes.

In which summary can you find each of the following problems? Write B or C on the line.

1. ___ The writer has not given the title of what is being summarized.

2. ___ The summary is too general; more specific information is needed.

3. ___ The summary has unnecessary details.

4. ___ The writer has not explained the main idea; instead, the summary is only a list of details from the story.

5. ___ The writer has included a personal opinion in the summary.

Activity 2 Write a one-paragraph summary of "The Monkey Garden" or "Red Clowns."

Points of Departure

1. In the United States, people disagree about whether it is all right for parents to hit their children. Some people feel that it is a normal part of teaching children how to behave; other people feel that it is never right. What is your opinion? Explain what you think, giving reasons and examples to support your ideas.

2. U.S. newspapers often feature advice columns, such as "Dear Abby" and "Ann Landers." Sometimes they are written especially for young people. Girls and boys write to the paper about problems in their lives, and the newspaper prints their letters with advice about what to do.

   Imagine that you are Sally and you have seen an advice column called "Ask Anna." Write a letter to Anna describing your situation and asking what to do. You can sign it with your name and your Mango Street address, or you can send it anonymously.

3. Describe a place you know well. Choose one that has a strong effect on you, whether it is a place you love or hate. To help your reader understand what this place is like, use details in your description that relate to one or more of the five senses: hearing, sight, touch, taste, and smell.

4. Esperanza's mother says she quit school because she didn't have nice clothes. Think about other times in the novel when we see how clothes influence people. Sometimes clothes are important to characters' feelings about themselves, and sometimes characters' clothes influence other people's attitudes towards them. Write about how clothes affect people, using examples from the novel to support your ideas.

5. In many ways, our lives are shaped by who our parents are. But our lives can also be very different from theirs. Esperanza's mother wants her daughter's life to be different from her own, and Esperanza wants this, too. What about you and your parents? In what ways do you want your life to be different from their lives? In what ways do you want it to be similar?

WORDS TO KNOW

* = irregular verb

PAGE

88 **settle** *(v.)* Esperanza's hair will **settle** when she gets older, her mother says.

tame *(adj.)*, Esperanza says she won't "grow up **tame**." She won't be like most girls.

lay *(v.)** Esperanza refuses to be like girls who "**lay** their necks on the threshold" and become prisoners.

89 **cruel** *(adj.)* In the movies, Esperanza has seen beautiful women who are **cruel** to men and drive them crazy.

92 **rub** *(v.)* Sally's mother **rubs** lard on the places where Sally has bruises from her father's beatings.

94 **take over** *(v.)** The neighborhood children **took over** the monkey garden for their playground.

95 **suppose** *(v.)* Esperanza **supposes** that she and her friends like the garden for the privacy it gives them.

96 **fist** *(n.)* Sally punched one of the boys with a soft **fist**.

grin *(v.)* Tito's buddies all **grinned** as they went into the garden with Sally to get their kisses.

97 **save** *(v.)* Esperanza felt that someone had to **save** Sally.

lie *(v.)** Esperanza **lay** down under a tree in the monkey garden and cried for a long time.

will *(v.)* Esperanza read that "in India there are priests who can **will** their heart to stop beating."

100 **sour** *(adj.)* A boy told Esperanza he loved her and pressed his **sour** mouth against her mouth.

tip *(v.)* To Esperanza, the sky seemed to **tip**.

Exercise 1 Write each word next to its definition.

      cruel   a fist   sour   tame

1. _____ with a sharp, acidic taste

2. _____ trained to be gentle

3. _____ the hand in a tightly closed position, as if to punch with it

4. _____ causing pain and suffering in others and enjoying it, merciless

Exercise 2 Use one of the following words or phrases to complete each sentence about the story. Change word forms as needed.

     rub   save   settle   suppose   take over   tip

1. Mama promised Esperanza that when she got older, her hair would _____ and not be so wild.

2. After Sally's father beat her, her mother would _____ lard into the places where she was hurt.

3. After the family with the monkey moved away, the neighborhood children _____ the garden behind their house.

4. Esperanza _____ that the reason they chose the garden was that it seemed almost a magical place.

5. After trying to get help from Tito's mother, Esperanza ran back to the garden to _____ Sally herself.

6. What happened to Esperanza by the tilt-a-whirl, when the sky seemed to _____?

Exercise 3 Use the same words to complete the following sentences, which are *not* related to the story. Change word forms as needed.

      rub   save   settle   suppose   take over   tip

1. I had to clean up a big mess after I accidentally _____ over my glass of juice.

2. The acting president of the college will be in charge until July 1; then the new president will _____.

3. It is the job of lifeguards to _____ swimmers from drowning.

4. I don't know what time it is, but I _____ it must be late because it's getting dark outside.

5. We _____ down comfortably on the couch to watch our favorite TV show.

6. I _____ so hard with my eraser that I tore the paper.

Exercise 4 What part of speech is the boldfaced word: *noun, verb,* or *adjective*?

1. _____ I realized he was only kidding when I saw the **grin** on his face.

2. _____ Do you trust him to tell us the truth? Do you think that he will **lie** to us?

3. _____ I don't think these apples are ripe yet; they have a **sour** taste.

4. _____ When he finally understood the joke, he **grinned** from ear to ear.

5. _____ The milk will **sour** if it is left out of the refrigerator for too long.

6. _____ Some people will tell a little white **lie** rather than hurt someone's feelings by telling the truth.

The verbs "lie" vs. "lay":

We have seen the verb "lie" used to mean "say something that is not true," as in "Sally, you lied" (99). "Lie" also has this meaning:

lie *(v.)** to be in a resting position (or put one's body down into a resting position)

present tense: lie, lies, lying
> She usually **lies** on the couch to watch TV.
> Whose book is **lying** on the floor?

past tense: lay
> She **lay** down and went to sleep.
> The money **lay** in the bank untouched for years.

past participle: lain
> I had just **lain** down for a nap when the phone rang.

The verb "lay" also has several meanings. One of them is similar to the meaning of "lie" given above:

lay *(v.)** to place or put (something) so it lies flat

present tense: lay, lays, laying
> I usually **lay** my keys on the table by the door.
> We're **laying** a new carpet in the living room today.

past tense: laid
> She **laid** her baby down to sleep.
> The cat **laid** a dead mouse on the mat outside the door.

past participle: laid
> I've **laid** my clothes on the bed; now I need to pack them into my suitcase.

Exercise 5 Read about **"lie"** and **"lay"** in the box on page 131. Which verb is correct in the following sentences? Circle it.

1. I usually **lie   lay** on the couch when I watch TV.

2. The tired student **lay   laid** her head on her desk.

3. He **lay   laid** down to rest after lunch.

4. I'm **lying   laying** your clean clothes on the bed.

Exercise 6 Fill in each blank with the appropriate form of **lie** or **lay**.

1. After he gave me the news, he _____ a hand gently on my shoulder.

2. Why are you still _____ in bed? Are you sick?

3. You can _____ your coat and hat over there.

4. He likes to _____ in bed until noon every Sunday.

5. Esperanza ran away from Sally and the boys and _____ down under a tree in the monkey garden.

> **will**
>
> a. *(v.)* to influence or control by the power of one's mind
>
> b. *(n.)* the strength of the mind to control one's actions
>
> c. *(n.)* a legal document that tells who will receive [someone's] money and property when that person dies
>
> From *The Newbury House Dictionary of American English*

Exercise 7 Look at the box above. Which meaning does "will" have in the following sentences? Write the letter of the definition next to each sentence.

_____ 1. My great-aunt left me $1,000 in her **will**.

_____ 2. The patient's condition grew worse, and he lost his **will** to live.

_____ 3. Esperanza tried to **will** her heart to stop beating.

✿ Part Nine ✿

Linoleum Roses
The Three Sisters
Alicia & I Talking on Edna's Steps
A House of My Own
Mango Says Goodbye Sometimes
About the Author
(pages 101–111)

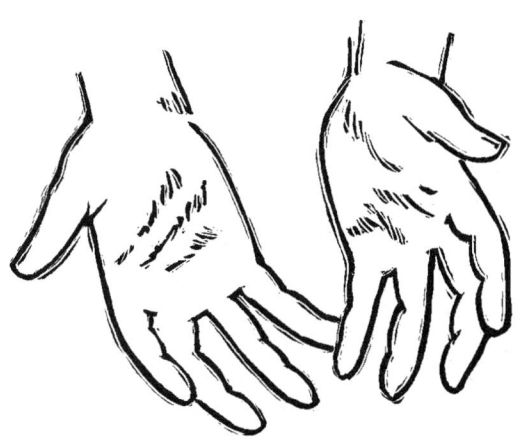

"Look at her hands, cat-eyed said . . . She's special" (104).

BEFORE YOU READ

PAGE

101   **a school bazaar =** a fair with games, food, and things for sale held to raise money for a school

   eighth grade (The average age of students entering eighth grade in the U.S. is 13.)

104   **she'll go very far** = she'll be very successful in life

105   **read my mind** = know what I was thinking

107   **Like it or not =** Whether you like it or you don't, the fact is …

111   **NEA fellowships** = National Endowment for the Arts awards

ON YOUR OWN

Reading

Read pages 101–110 without stopping.

A Closer Look

Linoleum Roses (pages 101–102)

1. Write a question about Sally to ask your classmates.

2. Write your opinion of Sally's marriage and your thoughts about her future.

The Three Sisters (pages 103–105)

3. Why do the three sisters come to Lucy and Rachel's house?

4. What responsibility does the sister "with marble hands" tell Esperanza she must remember?

Alicia & I Talking on Edna's Steps (pages 106–107)

5. How much time has passed since Esperanza moved into the house on Mango Street?

6. How does Esperanza feel about the house now?

A House of My Own (page 108)

7. What do you think is most important to Esperanza about having a house of her own?

Mango Says Goodbye Sometimes (pages 109–110)

8. Why does Esperanza write? Give two or more reasons, using not only what you read on pages 109–110 but also what you have learned about Esperanza throughout reading *The House on Mango Street*.

Write any questions *you* have about this part of the book.

SCENE FROM THE NOVEL

Create a script for reading aloud the conversation on pages 104–105 as you did in Part Four of the *Companion* (page 65).

1. Form a group of four. Each person will take a role and read the part of Esperanza or one of the three sisters: "Cat Eyes," "Blue Veins," or "Funny Laugh."

2. Open your books to page 104. Begin at the point where the three sisters call to Esperanza, "Come here." Underline the words spoken, and write the speaker's name in the margin, like this:

   <u>Cat Eyes</u> <u>What's your name</u>, the cat-eyed one asked.

   <u>ESP.</u> <u>Esperanza,</u> I said.

   <u>Blue Veins</u> <u>Esperanza,</u> the old blue-veined one repeated in a high thin voice. <u>Esperanza ... a good good name.</u>

3. Continue underlining the words spoken by each character and putting the speaker's name in the margin. The suggestions in the box below may help.

4. Before reading the scene aloud, each of you should practice your part by reading it softly to yourself.

Here is one way to interpret the scene:

Imagine that the three sisters are sitting side by side, first "Cat Eyes," then "Funny Laugh," and then "Blue Veins," followed by an empty chair.

When Esperanza first comes over to talk to the sisters, she stands facing them. "Funny Laugh," who is sitting in the middle, takes Esperanza's hands and turns them over as all three look at them and murmur to each other.

Sometimes more than one of the sisters talks at the same time. For example, all three sisters may say, "Yes, tomorrow" and "We know, we know."

When "Blue Veins" calls her aside, Esperanza sits down next to her in the empty chair and they speak privately.

The House on Mango Street

DISCUSSION

1. The three sisters tell Esperanza to make a wish. When she closes her eyes, what do you think she wishes for?

2. What does the sister "with marble hands" mean when she tells Esperanza "you must remember to come back" (105)?

3. Ask each other the questions you wrote about Sally from question 1 on page 136.

4. Esperanza says she won't come back to Mango Street "until somebody makes it better" (107). Who can make Mango Street better, and how can they do it?

5. Esperanza is, in many ways, Sandra Cisneros herself as a young girl. Read "About the Author" again (page 111) to learn something of what "Esperanza" did after leaving Mango Street.

   How has she kept her promise to go back "for the ones who cannot leave as easily"?

SUGGESTIONS FOR WRITING

Personal Response

Look back at your answer to the question on page 1 of the *Companion*, "How do you feel about reading a novel in English?" Reflect on your experience reading *The House on Mango Street*, and comment on the answer you wrote to that question. Have your feelings changed?

Summarizing

Write a summary of *The House on Mango Street*. It should be no more than 150 words.

Points of Departure

1. Write a letter to a new student in which you describe *The House on Mango Street*. Tell your reader whether or not you recommend the book and why.

   You could also make a poster advertising *The House on Mango Street* to go on a classroom or library wall. Draw it, paint it, design it on a computer, cut out magazine pictures for a collage, or use any combination of these techniques.

2. Reread the first part of the novel, pages 3–16. What impression of Esperanza do you get at the beginning of the book? By the end of the book, how has she changed? What has she learned? Describe the changes in Esperanza, and link them to the people and events that have influenced these changes.

3. Esperanza is not the only one who dreams of escaping from his or her present life: think of her father, Cathy, Marin, Alicia, Rafaela, and Sally. Choose three of these characters, or others from the novel, and describe how each one envisions "escape." How do they try to change their lives? Do you think they will succeed in escaping?

4. Imagine that you are one of the characters in the book who live on Mango Street. Esperanza has grown up and gone away, but you have kept in touch with her. Write her a letter telling her about what is happening in your life now.

5. *The House on Mango Street* takes place in a poor neighborhood in Chicago in the 1960's. Compare this neighborhood with what you know of poor city neighborhoods in the U.S. today. How are they the same as Esperanza's neighborhood? How are they different?

WORDS TO KNOW

* = irregular verb
PAGE

103   **fever** *(n.)* Lucy and Rachel's baby sister had a high **fever** and died.

104   **sense** *(v.)* Esperanza believes the three sisters had the power to **sense** things without being told about them.

complain *(v.)* The sister with the funny laugh **complained** that her knees hurt.

105   **selfish** *(adj.)* Esperanza thought that she had made a **selfish** wish, so she felt ashamed.

106   **undo** *(v.)** Esperanza says, "No, this isn't my house," and shakes her head as if she could **undo** her year on Mango Street.

109   **trudge** *(v.)* Esperanza tells a story in her head, describing herself **trudging** up the stairs to her house.

110   **ache** *(v.)* When Esperanza puts her memories down in writing, "then the ghost does not **ache** so much."

pack *(v.)* One day, Esperanza says, she will **pack** her books and papers and leave Mango Street.

111 **dropout** *(n.)*, **recruiter** *(n.)* Sandra Cisneros has been a teacher of high school **dropouts** and a college **recruiter**.

Exercise 1 Write each word next to its definition.

      an ache   **a dropout**   **a fever**   **selfish**

1. _____ someone who quits school

2. _____ a dull continuous pain

3. _____ thinking only of one's own interests, without concern for others

4. _____ an abnormally high body temperature

Exercise 2 Use one of the following words to complete each sentence about the story. Change word forms as needed.

      ache   **complain**   **pack**   **trudge**   **undo**

1. The sister with the funny laugh _____ that her knees hurt.

2. Esperanza shook her head "as if shaking could _____ the year" on Mango Street and erase it from her life.

3. When Esperanza told a story about herself in her head, she described how she _____ up the stairs of her house.

4. Writing stories and poems makes Esperanza feel better. When she puts her feelings down on paper, "the ghost does not _____ so much."

5. One day Esperanza will _____ her things and go away from Mango Street.

Exercise 3 Use the same words to complete the following sentences, which are *not* related to the story. Change word forms as needed.

> ache   complain   pack   trudge   undo

1. It's almost time to leave for the airport. Have you _____ your bags?

2. The expression "What is done, is done" means we can't erase what has happened, we can't _____ the past.

3. Some people are quick to speak up when someone's smoking bothers them; other people don't like to _____.

4. The mail carrier shouldered the heavy mailbag and _____ through the snow to deliver the mail.

5. The death of my friend made my heart _____.

NOUNS	VERBS	ADJECTIVES	ADVERBS
a recruiter _____ _____	_____		

Exercise 4 Use your dictionary to complete the chart above. Then fill in each blank with the appropriate member of this word family.

1. The army announced plans to increase its _____ of young women.

2. Someone who has just enlisted in the military is called a new _____.

3. Coaches of athletic teams at U.S. universities try to _____ talented high school athletes.

4. Sandra Cisneros worked as a college _____, trying to get young people to continue their education.

144   The ESL Reader's Companion

> **sense**
>
> a. (*n.*) a meaning or significance
>
> b. (*n.*) one of the five feelings of the body—sight, hearing, taste, smell, and touch
>
> c. (*n.*) intelligence, good judgment
>
> d. (*v.*) to be aware of
>
> From *The Newbury House Dictionary of American English*

Exercise 5 Look at the box above. Which meaning does "sense" have in each of these sentences? Write the letter of the definition next to each sentence.

_____ 1. She is a true friend, in every **sense** of the word.

_____ 2. If he had any **sense**, he wouldn't try such a dangerous trick!

_____ 3. The three sisters seemed to be able to **sense** things that were unspoken.

_____ 4. Esperanza thought the three sisters had a sixth **sense** and could see into her mind.

TEST YOURSELF

VOCABULARY REVIEW FOR PARTS 7, 8, AND 9

1. Are the meanings of the underlined words similar or different?

   _____ a. I'm all <u>through</u>.
   I'm all <u>finished</u>.

   _____ b. My back <u>aches</u>.
   My back <u>hurts</u>.

   _____ c. He <u>trudged</u> up the stairs.
   He <u>leaped</u> up the stairs.

   _____ d. They <u>took over</u> the President's office.
   They <u>tipped over</u> the President's office.

   _____ e. She is very <u>nosy</u>.
   She is very <u>wise</u>.

   _____ f. He <u>grinned</u> at me.
   He <u>stared</u> at me.

   _____ g. Don't be <u>cruel</u>.
   Don't be <u>mean</u>.

   _____ h. She is <u>raising</u> her children alone.
   She is <u>bringing up</u> her children alone.

2. Choose the best phrase to complete the sentence.

> . . . people's thoughts.
> . . . her heart to stop beating.
> . . . Sally from Tito and his friends.
> . . . her bags with books and papers.
> . . . the little pieces of paper with her poems.

a. Minerva used to **fold** _____.

b. Esperanza wanted to **save** _____.

c. Esperanza tried to **will** _____.

d. The three sisters could **sense** _____.

e. Esperanza planned to **pack** _____.

3. Unscramble each of these words. Their definitions follow.

a. riebtt = _ _ _ _ _ _ = having a sharp, biting taste, OR filled with anger, hate, and other bad feelings

b. teelts = _ _ _ _ _ _ = to become calm and orderly

c. scirtt = _ _ _ _ _ _ = severe, demanding

d. tuoprd = _ _ _ _ _ _ _ = someone who quits school

e. trecuir = _ _ _ _ _ _ _ = to get someone to join as a new member

f. pusopes = _ _ _ _ _ _ _ = to believe, think, assume

4. Use the clues given below to fill in the words in the puzzle.

ACROSS

4. an abnormally high body temperature
5. a state of mind or feelings
6. to put lightly into a liquid for a moment
7. to set something down so it lies flat
8. laughing or crying uncontrollably
11. domestic, trained, not wild or fierce
12. to press against something and slide back and forth

DOWN

1. thinking of oneself without care for others
2. to rest against something
3. a statement expressing dissatisfaction or annoyance
9. having a sharp and acidic taste
10. to be or put oneself in a resting position

All the words in the puzzle appear in this list:

bitterness	fever	lean	recruiter	takeover
bleed	fist	lie	rub	tame
complaint	hysterical	mood	selfish	tip
dip	lay	nosy	sour	undo

AFTERWORD

Is Sandra Cisneros "Esperanza"?

In her introduction to the tenth anniversary edition of the book, Sandra Cisneros writes,

> When I began *The House on Mango Street,* I thought I was writing a memoir. By the time I finished it, my memoir was no longer a memoir, no longer autobiographical. It had evolved into a collective story peopled with several lives from my past and present, placed in one fictional time and neighborhood—Mango Street (xi–xii).

Cisneros began writing the book in 1977 and finished it five years later. During that time, she taught Latino high school dropouts and counseled Latina students, and she found their lives, too, making their way into her book. So while *The House on Mango Street* began as her own story, it became the stories of other people as well. Cisneros writes,

> Am I Esperanza? Yes. And no. And then again, perhaps maybe (xix).

Self-Discovery

Sandra Cisneros has described how she made a discovery about herself that led to the writing of *The House on Mango Street.* At that time, she was 22 years old, a graduate student working towards a degree at the Iowa Writers Workshop. In her classes there, she had a strong and troubling sense of being different from her classmates and professors, of being odd and foreign. It made her feel ashamed and she stopped speaking in class.

Then came a class discussion of Gaston Bachelard's *Poetics of Space* and of houses as familiar and pleasurable sources of memories. Cisneros told interviewers Jussawalla and Dasenbrock,

> It was at that moment I realized, "I don't have a house—these things don't matter to me!" (*Laughter*) I don't have a house, how could I talk about house! With people from my neighborhood you'd be talking about a very different house than the one Bachelard was talking about—the wonderful house of memory. My house was a

prison for me; I don't want to talk about house (*Interviews with Writers*, 301–302).

After that class, Cisneros wrote a poem about an apartment, the start of a flood of poems and stories that were the beginnings of *The House on Mango Street*.

All of a sudden I realized, "Oh my God! Here's something that my classmates can't write about, and I'm going to tell you because I'm the authority on this—I can tell you" (ibid., 302).

Out of this realization came Cisneros's understanding that her differences could also be her strengths:

At that moment I ceased to be ashamed because I realized that I knew something that they could never learn at the universities. It was all of a sudden that I realized something that I knew I was the authority on.... It was the university of the streets, the university of life. The neighbors, the people I saw, the poverty that the women had gone through—you can't learn that in a class. I could walk in that neighborhood, and I knew how to walk in that neighborhood, and they didn't. So to me it began there, and that's when I intentionally started writing about all the things in my culture that were different from them (ibid., 302).

SUGGESTIONS FOR WRITING

1. You, too, are an authority, and you can write about what you know. For your eyes only, make a list of the things you know a great deal about. Include everything you can think of—don't leave things out because you aren't sure you want to write about them, or because you doubt anyone would want to read about them. List everything that comes to mind.

2. Cisneros writes, "At one time or another, we have all felt other" (*The House on Mango Street*, xv). She felt painfully different from her classmates and professors until she found the way to speak and write about her "otherness" as a woman, as a member of the working class, and as a Mexican-American.

   Have you ever had the experience of feeling different from—and not as good as—people you wanted to be with, people you wanted to accept you? What made you feel different? What did you do about it? How do you feel now about that experience?

3. An important part of American culture is the belief that anyone who is willing to work hard can change his or her life. The American idea is that people can shape their fates: while our lives are influenced by our families and the places where we are born, these factors do not control our futures.

   Do you think most people in your home culture share this belief? Do you believe in this idea? Or is it true for some people in some places but not for others? Explain what you think, giving your reasons for your beliefs.

ANSWER KEY

PART ONE

PAGE

14   *n.* = noun, *v.* = verb, *adj.* = adjective, *adv.* = adverb

16–20   **Exercises**

1. 1) a broom 2) a brick 3) even so 4) plenty
2. 1) even so 2) crumbling 3) pick 4) turn out 5) sobbing 6) inherited
3. 1) pick 2) crumbled 3) inherit 4) sobbed 5) turn out 6) even so
4. 1) swollen 2) ordinary 3) slippery
5. 1) verb 2) verb 3) noun 4) adjective
6. 1) robbery 2) robber 3) robbed
7. 1) robbed 2) stole 3) steal 4) stolen 5) robbed 6) robbed
8. 1) c, 2) a, 3) b
9. 1) b, 2) a, 3) b, 4) a, 5) a, 6) b

PART TWO

34–37   **Exercises**

1. 1) crooked 2) skinny 3) a load 4) an aisle
2. 1) grabber 2) chip in 3) find out 4) ahead 5) take turns 6) right away
3. 1) chipped in 2) grab 3) found out 4) right away 5) took turns 6) ahead
4. 1, 4, 6, and 7 are verbs; 2, 3, 5, and 8 are nouns
5. 1) float, float, float 2) slants, slant, slant 3) noticed, notice, notice 4) tug, tug, tugged
6. 1) c, 2) a, 3) b, 4) d

PART THREE

47   **Summarizing—Activity 2**

   1) B, 2) C, 3) C, 4) B

50–54   **Exercises**

1. 1) automatic 2) a blur 3) an alley 4) a siren 5) spit
2. 1) took off 2) get to 3) not know any better 4) dangle 5) gave up 6) simple
3. 1) dangle 2) simple 3) not know any better 4) take off 5) get to 6) give up
4. 1) blink 2) tough 3) fault
5. 1) imagines 2) imaginary 3) imagination 4) imaginative
6. 1) automatic, automatically 2) imaginatively, imaginative 3) simply, simple 4) wise, wisely

55–57   **TEST YOURSELF: PARTS 1 AND 2**

1. b) crumble in some places. c) turn out like the Vargas children. d) chip in to buy a bicycle. e) pick their sisters.
2. a) sob b) tug c) rob d) grab e) load f) peel g) broom h) slant i) notice j) find out
3. a) float b) aisle c) skinny d) crooked e) swollen f) forgive g) ordinary
4. a) the house on Mango Street b) Nenny's c) riding the bicycle d) Rachel and Lucy e) in the junk store

PART FOUR

70–73   **Exercises**

1. 1) jealous 2) strut 3) dizzy 4) puffy
2. 1) cute 2) kept on 3) scars 4) ashamed 5) dragged 6) show off
3. 1) ashamed 2) drag 3) Cute 4) scar 5) show off 6) kept on
4. 1) b, 2) a, 3) d, 4) c
5. 1) appreciate 2) appreciative 3) appreciation

6. 1) c, 2) b, 3) a
7. 1) b, 2) a, 3) c

PART FIVE

84–88 **Exercises**

1. 1) evil 2) authority 3) palm 4) a disease
2. 1) turn into 2) make fun of 3) making it up 4) spread 5) show up 6) crumpled
3. 1) made fun of 2) spread 3) showed up 4) turn into 5) make up 6) crumpled
4. *n.* = disgust, *v.* = disgust
   1) disgust 2) disgusted 3) disgusted
5. hug, imitate, make fun of
6. 1) noun 2) verb 3) verb 4) noun 5) noun 6) adjective
7. 1) a, 2) c, 3) b
8. 1) b, 2) a, 3) c

89–91 **TEST YOURSELF: PARTS 3 AND 4**

1. a, c, e, and f are similar; b, d, and g are different
2. a) get to wear nice clothes. b) imagine seeing mice. c) strut down the street together. d) drag her heavy feet across the floor. e) show off their new dance.
3. a) Marin b) Esperanza's mother c) Esperanza's mother d) Esperanza e) the Vargas children
4. ACROSS: 1) puffy 4) automatic 6) cute 8) blur 9) wise 10) dizzy
   DOWN: 2) fault 3) spit 5) ashamed 7) alley

PART SIX

101–104 **Exercises**

1. 1) a grip 2) a sigh 3) concrete 4) a surgeon
2. 1) notify 2) shrug 3) leap 4) prove 5) belong 6) droop
3. 1) prove 2) notified 3) shrug 4) drooped 5) leaped or leapt 6) belongs

4. 1) ferocious animals 2) a surgeon 3) mold 4) concrete
5. 1) b, 2) a, 3) d, 4) c
6. 1) c, 2) b, 3) a

PART SEVEN

113–116   **Exercises**

1. 1) mean 2) hysterical 3) strict 4) nosy
2. 1) dip 2) mood 3) lean 4) fold 5) were through 6) stared
3. 1) mood 2) stare 3) lean 4) dipped 5) were through 6) folded
4. 1) bloody 2) bled 3) blood
5. 1) c, 2) a, 3) b
6. 1) b, 2) a, 3) c

117–118   **TEST YOURSELF: PARTS 5 AND 6**

1. a) a disease b) a rock c) a car d) your education e) a lake
2. a) Esperanza b) Lucy and Rachel c) Esperanza, Lucy, and Rachel d) Aunt Lupe e) Elenita f) Geraldo
3. lied, showed up, shrugged, sighed (The other verbs are transitive; they require a direct object.)
4. a) deal b) evil c) mold d) droop e) prove f) shift g) spread h) imitate i) concrete j) ferocious

PART EIGHT

126   **Summarizing—Activity 1**

1) B, 2) B, 3) C, 4) C, 5) B

129–133   **Exercises**

1. 1) sour 2) tame 3) a fist 4) cruel
2. 1) settle 2) rub 3) took over 4) supposed 5) save 6) tip
3. 1) tipped 2) take over 3) save 4) suppose 5) settled 6) rubbed
4. 1) noun 2) verb 3) adjective 4) verb 5) verb 6) noun
5. 1) lie 2) laid 3) lay 4) laying

6. 1) laid 2) lying 3) lay 4) lie 5) lay
7. 1) c, 2) b, 3) a

PART NINE

143–145 **Exercises**

1. 1) a dropout 2) an ache 3) selfish 4) a fever
2. 1) complained 2) undo 3) trudged 4) ache 5) pack
3. 1) packed 2) undo 3) complain 4) trudged 5) ache
4. *n.* = a recruit, recruitment; *v.* = recruit
   1) recruitment 2) recruit 3) recruit 4) recruiter
5. 1) a, 2) c, 3) d, 4) b

146–148 **TEST YOURSELF: PARTS 7, 8, AND 9**

1. a, b, g, and h are similar; c, d, e, and f are different
2. a) the little pieces of paper with her poems. b) Sally from Tito and his friends. c) her heart to stop beating. d) people's thoughts. e) her bags with books and papers.
3. a) bitter b) settle c) strict d) dropout e) recruit f) suppose
4. ACROSS: 4) fever 5) mood 6) dip 7) lay 8) hysterical 11) tame 12) rub
   DOWN: 1) selfish 2) lean 3) complaint 9) sour 10) lie

TEACHING SUGGESTIONS

There are many ways that you, the instructor, might use this *Companion*. It is meant to be a versatile tool in your hands. Following are a few suggestions.

Starting Out

The questions in this section can help make you and the students aware of the ideas that each of you brings to the novel. Students can discuss the questions in small groups, or you can make this a Think/Pair/Share activity: Give the class a minute to think or write about a question, then have students pair off and share their ideas with their partners. Each pair then joins another pair, a larger group, or the whole class for follow-up. This technique enriches discussion and allows all the members of a class to take part.

Before You Read

Have the students read this section silently in class before beginning the reading assignment in the novel. They can then ask questions before doing the actual reading outside of class.

Reading Aloud   Reading aloud to your class at the beginning of the novel or a new part of it is an effective and pleasurable way to get students started on a reading assignment. Your reading aloud is also helpful if a passage confuses students because the stress and intonation you give to the passage may clarify its meaning for the students without your having to explain or interpret it.

The Novel on Tape   *The House on Mango Street* is available on audiocassette from Random House Audiobooks. Author Sandra Cisneros reads 30 of the 44 vignettes, presenting them in a somewhat different order from the book. The set of two tapes also features excerpts from Cisneros's *Woman Hollering Creek and Other Stories*. Order the tapes by calling (800) 733-3000 or by writing Random House Inc., Order Dept., 400 Hahn Rd., Westminster MD 21157.

On Your Own

Have the students write their answers to the questions in A Closer Look. Writing will consolidate their understanding of the material and help them sort out their thoughts about it. Depending on their level, you can urge, even require, that students use their own words rather than quotations.

Students can write their answers on separate sheets of paper to be handed in, or they can write them in the *Companion* for you to collect periodically.

If the students hand in written responses, you can scan their work quickly (while students begin freewriting or working in groups) to look for any major misconceptions about the novel or for questions students have written to you.

In class, review some of the questions in A Closer Look to lay a foundation for group discussion.

Scene from the Novel

On pages 65 and 138 of the *Companion* you will find instructions for dramatizing conversations from the novel. Students can read aloud from their scripts, taking the roles of the characters without the need to memorize their parts. These readings can be done in small groups, or volunteers can do them for the entire class. If students enjoy these, they can present conversations from other parts of the book, perform monologues, or act out scenes described in the book for which they write their own dialogue.

Discussion

You may wish to keep the entire class together for most discussions, particularly if there are fewer than ten students. Try the Think/Pair/Share technique described on page 157 under Starting Out.

In larger classes, small-group work promotes involvement in the discussion and helps foster in students an increased responsibility for their own learning. Groups of four or five students are generally small enough for students to manage and large enough to promise a variety of perspectives, particularly if you can set up groups that are mixed in terms of reading proficiency, English speaking skills, first language, and cultural background.

The need to produce something concrete, such as written answers to questions, and the prospect of reporting back to the class will give each group a clear purpose.

For balanced participation by all group members, have each student in a group be responsible for a particular role, with students changing roles at each meeting. Here are some suggested roles and their responsibilities:

- The Facilitator opens discussion, makes sure that each group member has an opportunity to speak, and sees that no one person dominates.
- The Recorder writes down the group's response(s) to each question.
- The Checker makes sure that members of the group understand each other and helps the Recorder as needed.
- The Timekeeper helps the group stay focused by keeping track of the time allotted for the discussion and the time they are spending on each question.
- The Spokesperson reports on what the group has discussed when the entire class reconvenes, referring if necessary to what the Recorder has written.

You can give each group a folder containing a handout describing these responsibilities and a sign-up sheet to help students keep track of the roles they assume.

Students must understand these roles well if they are to take them seriously and succeed in breaking out of patterns of group work in which a few students dominate. You can help by insisting that only the Recorder write on the group answer sheet and that only the Spokesperson speak for the group (until you open up discussion to everyone in the class), and by eliciting feedback from the students on their experiences in these roles.

For more information on Cooperative Learning, see *Learning Together and Alone* by David W. Johnson and Roger T. Johnson (1991, Allyn & Bacon) and *Cooperative Learning: Increasing College Faculty Instructional Productivity* by David W. Johnson, Roger T. Johnson, and Karl A. Smith (1991, The George Washington University).

Role-Plays The following ideas for role-plays do not require writing scripts or memorizing lines:

Panel: Have pairs of students assume the roles of characters. (Two students sharing one role may feel less pressured and generate more ideas and more talk.) Give the students a few minutes to discuss their character with their partner. Then have all the students sit in a circle or semicircle, partners together. Each pair in turn introduces themselves, and the other students ask them questions to answer in character.

Small-group interviews: Have several volunteers assume the roles of characters from the story. Let them leave the room (with their books) to talk over what they know and imagine about their characters. Lead the rest of the class in brainstorming questions to ask these characters, and write these sample questions on the board. Divide the class into small groups, preferably with three or four students, making as many groups as there are characters. Invite the role-players back into the room, asking each of them to join a group. Each group can then interview their character. Have the role-players change groups every few minutes.

Mingling: Give each student a slip of paper with a character's name on it. The student assumes the identity of that character. Everyone circulates around the room asking Yes/No questions of other students until they have enough information to guess the identities of the other students. Each student is allowed only one guess at the identity of each of the other characters.

Points of Departure

How you assign these topics will depend on your objective: If your goal is to develop students' fluency in written English and help them understand the reading, then use these topics for informal writing assignments, such as journal entries or freewriting in class. In these cases, you would address grammar and other aspects of accuracy only when the writer's meaning was obscured. (Note: Some of these topics are good for freewriting *before* students do the reading assignment.)

For more formal compositions, you will need to guide students through the stages of the writing process, from discussion of the assignment through prewriting, composing, sharing their drafts with you or their peers, revising, and editing. In order to maintain momentum in reading the novel, you can have the students carry such an assignment only partway through the process and then put aside their drafts until after they finish the novel. Then they can complete the revising and editing stages.

Words to Know

These exercises lend themselves to independent work by students. Once students have studied the vocabulary, review it in class. At the least demanding level: Ask students to open their *Companions* to a list of Words to Know and say, "Quickly, find a word that means . . ." or "Tell me a word that describes how Esperanza . . .." For a more demanding review: Post a list of the words on the wall or blackboard and ask students to speak about the meaning of each word and its use in the story.

The emphasis in the vocabulary exercises is on developing students' *understanding* of words they read. The students will need additional practice and guidance to be able to *use* the words in speaking and writing.

Assessment

Possibilities include:

Requiring portfolios based on the novel: Portfolios can include homework assignments, journal entries, in-class writing, essays, samples of group work, and the student's reflections on the process of reading the novel with the class.

Giving quizzes on the novel: Quizzes can include vocabulary exercises (which may be taken directly from the *Companion*); short-answer questions about events and relationships; exercises on matching quotations and the characters who spoke the lines or are described in them; and lists of important people, places, and things from the novel for students to identify.

Having students create tests: Groups of students can make up questions about the novel to hand in to you. Choose questions from each group to create a test.

Giving an open-book exam: Give students a choice of essay topics (which may be drawn from the Discussion or Points of Departure sections of the *Companion*). They should find support in the novel for statements they make and include page references in their essays.

WORDS TO KNOW

All the words included under Words to Know are listed here. *Companion* page numbers are given in parentheses.

A
ache (142)
ahead (33)
aisle (33)
alley (48)
appreciate (69)
ashamed (69)
authority (82)
automatically (48)

B
be through (with) (112)
belong (100)
bitter (111)
bleed (112)
blink (49)
blur (49)
brick (14)
broom (14)

C
chip in (32)
complain (142)
concrete (101)
crooked (32)
cruel (128)
crumble (14)
crumple (83)
cute (68)

D
dangle (49)
deal (100)
dip (112)
disease (83)
disgusted (83)
dizzy (69)

drag (69)
droop (101)
dropout (143)

E
even so (14)
evil (83)

F
faint (69)
fault (49)
ferocious (100)
fever (142)
find out (32)
fist (128)
float (33)
fold (112)
forgive (16)

G
get to (49)
giggle (33)
give up (49)
grab (32)
grin (128)
grip (100)

H
hug (84)
hysterical (111)

I
imagine (49)
imitate (84)
inherit (16)
invisible (68)

J
jealous (68)

K
keep on (68)

L
lay (127)
lean (112)
leap (100)
lie (83, 128)
limp (84)
load (33)

M
make fun of (82)
make (something) up (83)
mean (111)
mold (100)
mood (112)

N
nosy (112)
not know any better (49)
notice (33)
notify (99)

O
ordinary (15)

P
pack (142)
palm (84)
peel (15)
pick (15)
plenty (15)
prove (100)

puffy (68)
punch (33)

R
raise (112)
recruiter (143)
right away (33)
rob (15)
rub (128)

S
save (128)
scar (68)
selfish (142)
sense (142)
settle (127)
shame (99)
shift (83)
show off (69)
show up (83)
shrug (100)
shy (69)
sigh (100)
simple (50)
since (15)
siren (48)
skinny (32)
slant (34)
slippery (15)
sob (15)

sour (129)
spit (49)
spread (83)
stare (112)
strict (111)
strut (69)
suppose (128)
surgeon (99)
swollen (14)

T
take off (48)
take over (128)
take turns (33)
tame (127)
tip (129)
tough (50)
trade (68)
trudge (142)
tug (32)
turn into (82)
turn out (15)

U
undo (142)

W
will (128)
wise (50)

Notes